Lights, camera . . . action

The film clip that Kyle had chosen for their talk show had one of the hottest young actors in America making magic with an equally sexy young actress.

Watching, Amanda moaned inwardly, squirming in her chair. She tried to remember that she was cohosting this half-hour fiasco, that she and Kyle were supposed to be on opposing sides of the "what's sensual" debate. At the moment, she was feeling very much in tune with him.

She looked up then and caught his eyes on her. He mouthed the words "hot stuff, huh?" and winked. Amanda had a feeling his mind wasn't on the images moving on the screen. . . .

The clip ended. "Now, Amanda," Kyle challenged her, "on behalf of our appreciative audience, I dare you to tell me *that* scene didn't turn you on."

Who cared if millions were watching? Then and there, Amanda could have shown him how turned on she was . . . to him!

Dear Reader:

Nothing is more intriguing than a letter from a secret admirer. But what if a man received a series of anonymous, deliciously scented letters, complete with provocative suggestions? Intrigued wouldn't begin to describe his response.

This letter to you, the prospective reader of *Open Invitation*, urges you to let yourself be transported into a woman's world of romance and sensual fantasy... where a lively imagination is the only compass... and the only boundary. Temptation has never been sexier.

Tiffany White's *Open Invitation*. We couldn't help but succumb and make it an Editor's Choice. Would it have been your choice, too? We eagerly await your reaction.

Harlequin Temptation Editors

225 Duncan Mill Road
Don Mills, Ontario
Canada
M3B 3K9

Open Invitation
TIFFANY WHITE

Harlequin Books

TORONTO • NEW YORK • LONDON
AMSTERDAM • PARIS • SYDNEY • HAMBURG
STOCKHOLM • ATHENS • TOKYO • MILAN

For my husband
and the three
magic kisses of
Lust, Love and Laughter

Published November 1989

ISBN 0-373-25374-5

1

"YOU DO REALIZE, Miss Butterworth, that Kyle Fox is going to want a cohost about as much as a Texas oilman wants a Yankee son-in-law?" Noah Trent, the bald station manager of KCNX television, asked, leveling a considering stare at the young woman sitting before him.

Amanda Butterworth had heard all the rumors about Kyle Fox. Had heard all about his hotshot personality and heart-stopping good looks. No doubt the perks of hosting *Theater Talk* suited him just fine: he didn't have to work too hard, he made lots of money and he was crotch-deep in female fans.

Still, *Theater Talk*'s ratings had begun to slip, or Noah Trent wouldn't be entertaining the idea of hiring her.

She slid her elegantly manicured hands back and forth in her lap. Her palms were clammy and she was as pale as her pastel hose. "Yes sir, but . . ." she began in a voice whispering of her attendance at a fancy eastern girls' school.

Noah held up his large hand to halt her as he flipped open the folder she'd handed him containing the scripts of her on-screen movie reviews.

While she waited for him to finish scanning them, her heart pounded in her ears. The deep calming breath she took didn't relax her as she'd hoped. Nervously, she reached to toy with a tawny tendril escaping from her sleek French braid. Her terrible shyness was the reason she'd forced herself into a career in front of the camera. The camera had since become her friend, and she'd conquered her shyness. She was only nervous now because she so desperately wanted the job.

The station manager finally closed the folder on his desk and looked up to study the young woman in front of him. The room was silent except for the drum of his fingers on the top of the folder. "You do good work, Miss Butterworth," he finally said.

Amanda's padded shoulders relaxed a fraction at his compliment, but her posture remained straight and proper.

"However..." Noah began, pushing back his scarred swivel chair to get up.

Amanda's breathing stopped. He'd changed his mind! He wasn't going to give her the job.

But he didn't offer her his hand. Instead, he turned his back to her and walked over to the window and looked out at the dark clouds scuddering across the gray sky above the riverfront. She let out her breath on a tremble of relief. Maybe she could still persuade him.

Before she got the chance, there was a rap on the office door, and a young intern came in on Noah's bellowed invitation.

"Yes, Toby, what is it?" he asked, turning to the curly haired young man who'd knocked.

"Uh...sir...Mr. Fox just called in," Toby answered, clearing his throat nervously. "He said he won't be able to make the staff meeting you called for this afternoon."

Noah glowered at the intern. "Did he say *why* he doesn't deem it necessary to honor us with his presence?"

"Uh...he mentioned something about being tired...and needing some time off for relaxation...." The intern's voice trailed off, and he took an unconscious step backward.

Noah turned back to the window and gazed longingly at a barge working its way upriver as he rubbed his stomach with two fingers.

Amanda suspected an ulcer. As station manager of KCNX television, he dealt with a lot of egos.

She had been elated when Noah had called her and asked her to come in to discuss a staff addition he was considering. He'd mentioned liking what he'd seen of her movie-review segment on the local news when he'd been in her city on business.

It would be a great career opportunity for her to move to the larger market at KCNX. She was sure she could do the job. She hadn't been sure how Kyle Fox would take to the idea of a partner. Noah had just made that more than plain.

She wasn't going to let him ruin this golden opportunity she was being offered. Plainly, Noah thought Kyle needed someone to shake up his complacency, or he wouldn't have contacted her.

"Get hold of Kyle and tell him I want to see him in my office, *now*," Noah commanded.

"Yes sir," the intern answered, hurrying off to make the call.

Deep in thought, Noah Trent continued staring out the window, seeming to have forgotten Amanda was still in his office.

Taking a deep breath, Amanda seized the initiative. "I really want this job, Mr. Trent."

Noah turned and looked at her doubtfully. Sliding his hand over his smooth bald head, he began voicing his concerns. "I know you're good at handling your job," he said, "but how good are you at handling men?"

Amanda's hand went to tug at the cameo pinned on the frothy white lace jabot at the collar of her ivory linen blouse. "Excuse me?" she asked, taken aback by his question until she realized Noah was judging her by her professional attire. He was assuming she was as prim and proper as she appeared, incorrectly assuming she'd never had a lover and was inexperienced when it came to men.

Returning to his chair and leveling his gaze directly on her, Noah said, "To be perfectly frank, Miss Butterworth, doing this job means you'll have to handle working with Kyle Fox. Kyle is a man who likes to get his way, and he'll cajole you with his charm or romance you with his looks to get it."

"I assure you I can handle Mr. Fox," Amanda vowed. If he thought she'd be putty in Kyle Fox's hands, he was wrong.

Noah considered her. A fire had flashed briefly in her eyes. So there *was* more to Miss Butterworth than the prim and proper facade would indicate. "You know," he said, a bit amazed, "I'm beginning to believe you could."

Amanda took a deep breath. "Then I have the job?"

Noah reached for the dish of hard candy on his desk. Taking a peppermint for himself, he offered the dish of candy to Amanda.

"No, thank you," she declined, growing increasingly impatient as he took his time uncrinkling the cellophane wrapping around the candy.

"I just quit smoking," Noah said, plopping the sweet into his mouth.

Amanda tried to smile through gritted teeth, afraid she was going to scream if he didn't answer her question soon.

"If I give you the job of cohosting *Theater Talk* with Kyle, how would you go about raising the ratings?" Noah hedged, moving the peppermint to one side with his tongue.

There was no hesitation in Amanda's voice. "By giving you something Mr. Fox can't give you working alone."

Noah steepled his fingers. "I hesitate to ask. Alone he's given me ulcers and indigestion."

Amanda jumped into the opening Noah gave her. "Controversy, Mr. Trent. You put Mr. Fox and me together, reviewing the same movies, and I guarantee you'll have controversy."

"Controversy. . . ." Noah toyed with the idea.

Amanda pushed the sale. "Controversy sparks interest. Interest sparks viewers. The more controversy, the more viewers. The more viewers, the higher the ratings. You mentioned you'd gotten the idea for two movie reviewers from the success of Siskel and Ebert. They often disagree over films but not as much as a man and a woman would, or at least not as much as Mr. Fox and I will."

As Noah leaned forward in his chair, its springs seemed to squeak in relief. Staring hard at Amanda, he asked, "What makes you so sure?"

Amanda was waiting for him, her nervousness at bay when caught up in the business of discussing her career. When it came to having faith in her opinions and feelings in her personal life, she was less confident. Her career, however, was another matter. When talking about her work, she could back up her opinions cold. It was her area of real strength. It was why it was so important for her to succeed.

"After you called, I made it my business to preview tapes of *Theater Talk*. If you'll excuse me for saying so, your Mr. Fox is the closest thing to a Neanderthal walking upright today. I can assure you, sir, there is little, if anything, Mr. Fox and I agree on," she promised, her green eyes flashing.

Noah massaged his stomach again. "I don't know, Miss Butterworth. . . ."

Amanda wasn't having any of it. No way was he going to deny her this chance to move into a larger market from the small station where she currently worked. Her argument was on target. She knew it and he knew it. She pressed her advantage. "Besides, Mr. Trent, with me as backup, you'll have something to hold over Mr. Fox's *attitude*."

Noah nodded, but he still played hardball. "Okay, you've got yourself a shot, Miss Butterworth—thirteen weeks. But if at the end of thirteen weeks, you haven't shown me a ratings gain, you're out."

"You won't be sorry, sir," Amanda promised, allowing herself a smile for the first time since the interview had begun. She knew smiles put women at a disadvantage in business dealings with men.

"Maybe," Noah commented, noncommittal about her promise. "I am sure about one thing, though," he added, his eyes alive with anticipation. "It's going to be worth risking the thirteen weeks just to see the look on Kyle's face when I tell him he's going to have a cohost."

After discussing station policy briefly, Noah penciled in a set of figures on a standard thirteen-week contract. Amanda reached for the paper he slid across his desk for her approval. The penciled sum was enough to cover her expenses for thirteen weeks, though she was certain it wouldn't even cover Kyle's florist bill.

It wasn't the money that annoyed her. It was Kyle's reputation. Industry rumor indicated he went through women like a debutante goes through party dresses—and with about as much attachment. Evidently the word *relationship* wasn't in his vocabulary. How was she going to form a working relationship with a man like him? It was his problem, she decided finally. She was his cohost whether he liked it or not.

Amanda nodded her agreement to Noah's penciled sum.

There was a knock at the door again. "Come in," Noah called out.

It was the intern who had interrupted earlier. "There's a call from your wife on line three, sir."

Noah snapped his fingers. "That's right, she's at some clothing designer's trunk showing at the mall."

Turning to the intern, Noah said, "Toby, Miss Butterworth is going to be joining KCNX as a movie reviewer for *Theater Talk*. Show her the studio where the show is taped and give her the usual employment forms to fill out."

"Yes sir."

As an aside to Amanda, he added, "I'll have the contract typed up for you as soon as I take this call from my wife. Oh, and Toby—I almost forgot. Did you get hold of Mr. Fox?"

"Yes. He's on his way in, sir." The curiosity alive in the young intern's eyes asked the question he didn't dare to: Is he also on his way out?

Noah took mercy on the kid and satisfied his curiosity. It was going to be common knowledge shortly, anyway. "Miss Butterworth and Mr. Fox are going to be working together as partners on *Theater Talk*."

Amanda watched a glowing anticipation replace the curiosity in Toby's eyes. It was obvious he thought things were going to get real interesting around KCNX. Toby, however, refrained from commenting.

He followed Noah's instructions and gave Amanda a quick tour of the studio. That done, he then settled her at a vacant desk outside Noah's office with a sheaf of forms to fill out and the typed contract needing her signature.

Amanda bent her head to search through the plastic cards in her wallet for her driver's license. She hated filling out forms. For some reason she had a mental block and could never remember the sequence of the last four numbers on her social security card.

Her head was still bent at her task when she heard a door open in the corridor, then slam shut, followed by the sound of determined footsteps. She didn't look up, but she had a limited view from the corner of her eye.

Flat-heeled, soft white leather boots with tooled silver at the toe and heel marched by. Her field of vision extended to the hem of a long, white denim cowboy duster swirling out behind the wearer, trailing the alluring scent of a freshly showered man. When he'd gone several feet past her, she glanced up to also see the wearer had the rangy height and breadth of shoulders to carry off the duster coat. Her glance moved up to take in his trademark moussed and precision-cut longish dark blond hair. Even from the back, there was no mistaking Kyle Fox. He'd finally made it into the television station.

Turning the knob, he marched right into Noah Trent's office unannounced.

Amanda wished she had Kyle's easy confidence. Only a man who had enormous self-assurance dressed the way he pleased, even when it made him stand out in a crowd. Amanda would love to wear the kind of contemporary, sexy clothes Kyle wore so effortlessly. Instead, she worried about what people would think and settled for safe.

For the next ten minutes the muffled sounds coming from Noah Trent's office unnerved Amanda. An argument was plainly raging between Noah and Kyle. The door to Noah's office rattled with all the yelling. Amanda hated yelling. Her father had yelled. He had been a demanding man, and her mother had been devoted to pleasing him. Her parents had been so absorbed with each other, she'd always felt like the odd one out.

To compensate, she'd lived in the fantasy world she'd invented from the movies that were her escape. She'd spent much of her childhood watching and wishing, leaving her shy and unsure of her feelings and opinions in the real world.

The muffled noises coming from Noah's office stopped finally, and as she waited with her hands folded on top of her completed employment forms, the door opened and Noah leaned out.

"Miss Butterworth, would you come into my office, please? Oh, and bring those forms with you."

When Amanda rose, she was a nervous wreck. She hadn't counted on being present when Kyle Fox found out he had to share *Theater Talk* with a cohost.

She laid the forms on Noah's desk. Her legs felt like jelly, and there was a faint buzzing in her head. She quickly took the nearest chair.

Noah began studying the forms, giving Kyle and Amanda a chance to study each other. Except they didn't.

Kyle continued to lounge at the window, his weight on one leg, his hands braced on the soffit above his head as he stared out across the river.

Amanda didn't have to look at him to know he was there. His sexual charisma was a living force in the room. To her dismay, her body was responding to it.

After a few long moments, Noah looked up. Smiling, he put Amanda's signed contract and employment forms in an interoffice envelope and placed them in the Out basket on the corner of his cluttered desk. "I'm sorry. Where are my manners? Miss Butterworth, the gentleman over by the window, contemplating jumping, is Kyle Fox."

Amanda couldn't escape turning to look at Kyle without being impolite. While she never let anyone take advantage of her, she was hardly ever impolite. Her green eyes moved past the white denim duster Kyle had discarded on the old tweed sofa against the wall and came to rest on his profile. He had the kind of sexy slouch that was the staple of cigarette and motorcycle ads.

The right knee was out of his well-worn jeans, and the waistband stood out a bit from his starched white tuxedo shirt, evidencing a belly that was as lean and flat as a boxer's.

Any thought of her new job disappeared from her mind to be replaced by thoughts that were carnal and lascivious. She wanted to unbutton his starchy white shirt and explore what her mind imagined. She wanted to feel . . . No, enough of this, she scolded.

Still, despite her stab at control, she couldn't resist a few seconds more of perusal. Nice, long, muscular thighs and tight buns. There was nothing loose about his jeans there, or for that matter—

Noah coughed.

With a start, Amanda realized she'd drifted into intimate scrutiny. All those long hours in darkened movie theaters had made her prone to fantasizing. Even though Noah couldn't have seen her visual survey, she was mortified. What if Kyle had turned his attention from the view outside the window and caught her?

"Kyle, I want you to meet Amanda Butterworth," Noah said.

Kyle turned. Surely Noah wasn't serious! he thought. She looked so . . . so repressed. That prim and proper suit of hers was positively disgusting. At least Noah could have given him a sexy cohost.

Amanda was distressed to find his masculine appeal was easily double in person as he ambled toward her. He had the easy walk of a man who rides astride-motorcycles, horses, whatever.

Amanda rose to take his offered hand. His touch, though he did nothing overt, was alarmingly intimate. Instinctively she tried to pull back. Pulling back from her feelings was second nature to her.

Giving way was obviously not second nature to him. His grip tightened and so did her stomach.

She saw three things up close; none of them really a surprise. The first two, she was already aware of from previewing tapes of *Theater Talk*: he had eyes so blue they ought to be illegal and a sexy cleft in his squared chin. She might have guessed at number three from his thick mane of hair. Dark blond chest hair in the same abundance curled in the open neck of the tuxedo shirt and on his forearms, bared below the turned-back sleeves.

All three things were unnerving, but it wasn't until he decided to replace his scowl with a smile that she knew she was really in trouble. Knew without a doubt, Kyle Fox was going to be way more than she had bargained for.

His smile made her feel as if he'd just placed his warm hand on her lower abdomen, his long fingers spread wide. She felt it so profoundly that she couldn't control her quick, involuntary intake of breath. Her cheeks and the tip of her nose turned pink as alarming feelings of arousal rushed and flowed over her like a waterfall.

Kyle noted her reaction and seemed pleased. Real pleased. Too pleased, if you asked her.

While his teeth were close to perfect, the slant of his smile suggested thoughts that were anything but. She had just been served notice that Kyle Fox was a squeaky-clean man with a very dirty mind.

Unlike Amanda, who liked to keep her vices hidden, he bought the Madison Avenue slogan that it pays to advertise.

Noah remained as quiet as a monk's prayer, his shrewd brown eyes watching them take each other's measure.

Kyle's mood had gone from black to sunny.

The look in Amanda's eyes mirrored that of a deer caught in an oncoming vehicle's headlights.

Kyle took his time releasing her hand. Maybe having her as his cohost wouldn't be so bad, after all, he decided. Better to have some sweet little impressionable thing than a shrewd, savvy competitor.

Stepping back, he finally released her hand and began a slow, thorough perusal of her. Beginning with the prim and proper pumps adorning her feet, his blue gaze moved to take in the stingy amount of leg she was showing in her pastel hose beneath her midcalf skirt, then traveled to her conservative matching jacket and the frilly linen blouse beneath, covering her from wrist to throat.

He raised his fingertips to his lean hips. Mischief began to twinkle in his baby blues as he took in her colorless lip gloss and her severe French braid.

"Don't tell me, let me guess," he said, planting his tongue firmly in his cheek. "You're the network censor, right?"

2

KYLE SLID HIS SUNGLASSES down from the top of his head and hid behind them, smug and unrepentant.

"Your attitude is only confirming Miss Butterworth's opinion of you," Noah warned.

"Her opinion?" She had opinions. That wasn't a good sign.

Amanda remembered describing Kyle as a Neanderthal and groaned inwardly.

"Miss Butterworth seems to think . . . you're rude, crude and socially unacceptable."

Kyle lifted his sunglasses back on top of his head and stared hard at Amanda. The corners of his lips twitched. "I'll bet."

There was that warm hand on her abdomen again, and he knew it. It took all of Amanda's willpower not to squirm under the suggestive glint in Kyle's intense stare. Finally taking the coward's way out, she averted her eyes.

"Miss Butterworth is going to cohost *Theater Talk* with you on a trial basis for the next thirteen weeks. I want to see if we can stop the slide in *Theater Talk*'s ratings by creating a little controversy," Noah said, getting down to the business at hand. "We'll be switching to the same format Siskel and Ebert use, with the two of you sharing equal time. We'll review four movies a week, and when you get adjusted to working with each other, we'll try some new ideas."

Turning to Amanda, Noah said, "Instead of screening the films alone ahead of time, Kyle prefers to see them as they're released to the theaters. That way, he sees the films with the theater audience, under the same conditions they experience. The viewers seem to like it, so we'll continue with Kyle's system—"

"Excuse me, sir," Amanda interrupted, voicing her objection. "I don't know if I can view a film with an audience and not let the audience's reaction influence my review. I don't see how I can remain objective."

"You can if you're a professional," Kyle challenged. "I do it all the time. In fact, I'm sometimes the only person in the theater who likes a film. I say so in my reviews. That's how I created controversy, and very successfully, I might add, without needing any partner."

Noah nodded. "I have to agree with Kyle. We'll give it a try his way. If it doesn't work for you after you've tried it for a while, then we'll discuss it."

Kyle was enjoying his little victory, when Noah turned his attention to him.

"And, Kyle, it wouldn't hurt for the two of you to occasionally attend the same screenings. It could garner us good free publicity for the show."

"Not if they see me killing her, it wouldn't," Kyle muttered under his breath, then turned and smiled sweetly at her.

Noah reached into his top right-hand drawer for his bottle of antacid tablets and shook out a couple. "Kyle, I expect you to cooperate with Miss Butterworth. Show her the ropes around here, get her fixed up with theater passes, and then take her with you to a screening tomorrow."

Walking to retrieve his white duster from the sofa, Kyle asked, "Is that all, Noah . . . or do you have some more good news for me?" Having a cohost foisted on him hadn't made his day.

Noah tossed down the paper clip he'd been twisting and leaned back in his chair precariously. "No, that's all. I'll even let you skip the staff meeting, if you promise to extend Miss Butterworth every courtesy."

As he shrugged into his cowboy duster, Kyle pulled his boyish smile out of storage. He couldn't resist needling her.

"How 'bout if I take her shopping and jazz up her image a little? She's going to have to show a little leg if she wants the . . . uh . . . ratings to rise."

"I'll show a little leg when you show a little leg," Amanda mumbled between clenched teeth.

Kyle flashed her a grin, showing he was beyond redemption.

"Kyle, I mean it. I expect you to make Miss Butterworth's trial period as pleasant as possible," Noah warned.

Kyle removed his sunglasses from the top of his blond head and flashed Amanda a sexy wink before sliding them on. His voice was all husky promise. "Noah, I'll be so pleasant, Miss Butterworth will pure miss me when she's out on her prim little bottom at the end of her thirteen weeks." Picking up a peppermint from Noah's desk, Kyle shot her a look that was so confident it was insulting.

Amanda was furious that Kyle Fox knew she found him attractive despite their differences. She longed for a way to make it mutual. Fat chance, she thought, recalling how much her prim and proper appearance amused him. At least she had a fighting chance to hold her own careerwise, she consoled herself. That would have to be enough; anything else was plain wishful thinking.

Toby knocked, then came in to announce there was another call on line two from Noah's wife.

"That's all for now," Noah said, motioning them outside his office so he could take the call in private.

In the corridor, Amanda bent to get a drink at the water fountain, then turned and watched as Toby stopped to tell Kyle a joke that made him laugh. His laugh was wicked and did unsettling things to her equilibrium. Toby left and Amanda's gaze lingered, watching Kyle as he unwrapped the piece of hard candy from Noah's candy dish.

He looked up and caught her watching.

Her heart thudded against her ribs, and she gasped softly as his eyes imprisoned her.

Deliberately rewrapping the piece of candy, he headed toward her. As he stalked her, Amanda found herself backing away until she came up against a wall.

Straight-arming her so that she was trapped against the wall between his arm and the water fountain, he lifted her chin with his fingertip. Lowering his mouth to within an inch of hers, he whispered, "I feel like something sweet. How 'bout it, Amanda, are you as sweet as you look?"

Her eyes narrowed as he lowered his lips to hers and took her breath away.

When he was good and ready, he pushed himself back, his hand still braced on the wall near her head, trapping her.

Unprepared to resist, she hadn't. But she had managed the hard-won victory of a minimal response.

Kyle's smile was gently mocking as he shook his head. "Nope, that was a little *too* sweet. We're going to have to work on it."

There was a brash promise in the blue depths of his eyes as he pushed away from the wall, unwrapped the piece of candy still in his hand, plopped it into his mouth and ambled away whistling.

Whistling!

Without thinking, Amanda headed after him. There was no way she was going to let him walk away unscathed and complacent. If they were going to work together, it was best they got the ground rules straight between them at the outset.

"Just one minute, mister!" she called, finally catching up to him.

Kyle turned at the sound of her voice.

"That's okay, you can call me Kyle," he said, teasing and unrepentant, though he wished she wasn't such an easy target.

"What was that supposed to be back there?" she demanded, ignoring his witty rejoinder.

"What?" he asked, spreading his hands wide, palms up in a perfect pretense of innocence. He was beginning to enjoy himself.

"You know perfectly well *what*," she answered, waiting for his response.

He shrugged. "What did it feel like?" he asked, his eyes journeying over her lazily, his smile provocative.

"I'll tell you what it felt like," she fumed. "It felt like intimidation. Don't try it again."

"Yes ma'am." She had spirit. This might even be fun.

"That's okay, you can call me Amanda," she replied tartly, tossing back his rejoinder as she turned on her heel.

Kyle caught her arm, stopping her.

"Amanda?"

"What?"

"Welcome aboard," he said, the words a thick, sensuous whisper.

She clamped her eyes closed against the rush his words gave her, willing away their easy seduction. As she walked away, a line from a favorite old movie played in her head.... "Fasten your seat belts. It's going to be a very bumpy ride."

NIGHTFALL FOUND AMANDA in her motel room, tossing and turning restlessly in the strange bed. The mattress was too soft and the pillows were too hard, but they weren't the cause of her wakefulness.

True, she was excited about her new position, but that wouldn't have kept her from sleeping, either.

Kyle Fox was the culprit responsible for the adrenaline wiring her nerves. What Noah had warned her of was true. Kyle would use his charm and good looks to get his way. The awful part was she was more than a little susceptible to both.

She was vulnerable and off balance. What she needed was a way to get Kyle off balance, as well. A way to get even with him for toying with her and not taking her seriously. A way to get to him.

Throwing back the covers, she got up and turned on the television, flipping through the channels for something diverting to relax her.

She'd seen the three movies showing on the cable channels, the talk show had a pompous guest, and she wasn't in the mood to shop or buy the real estate the two other channels were pitching. She settled on a music channel.

Before long the images began to blur as her mind found a diversion all its own. Kyle Fox's image appeared before her wearing the same snug jeans and tuxedo shirt he'd worn into the station, only now she gave her imagination free rein as she began undoing the buttons of his tuxedo shirt . . .

"I'M GOING TO KILL HIM!" Amanda muttered as she paced back and forth in the lobby of her motel the next afternoon, waiting for Kyle to pick her up. He was already a half hour late, and there was still no sign of him on the horizon.

She looked down at her watch for the tenth time in as many minutes and stifled a yawn. Her emotions had been on a roller coaster ride since yesterday. She'd started out a little anxious over the interview with Noah Trent, then had been excited when Noah had hired her as Kyle's cohost despite his second thoughts. Kyle's arrival had been both exciting and scary in a fascinating sort of way.

Never had a man been so, as Noah Trent had put it, "rude, crude and socially unacceptable" to her . . . and so damned attractive at the same time. She knew she should despise him. It annoyed her that she desired him, instead. Him and his hot looks and cool stares that touched secret places and hidden feelings.

Per Noah's instructions, Kyle had arranged for the two of them to attend a screening together today. Kyle had insisted on picking her up. The movie they were going to see was due to start in half an hour. Any kind of minor traffic snarl and they would be late for the movie. She didn't know about Kyle, but she took her job seriously and considered it unprofessional to review a movie that was already in progress.

She was on her way to the pay phone to call him when she heard the sound of a horn blasting at the entrance to the motel. Turning at the sound, she looked through the glass doors to the street and saw Kyle leaning against the fender of a Mustang convertible, circa '65. Both car and man looked in mint condition. Maybe she wouldn't kill him, after all.

He had on his sunglasses, and she supposed she ought to be ashamed that what she recognized was the jut of his hip and the fit of his jeans. He had traded in his white denim duster of yesterday for a brown leather bomber jacket, so the view was unspoiled.

Unlike the man, she thought with chagrin as she hurried to join him. It probably wasn't his fault he was spoiled. Women, no doubt, stood in line for the chance to spoil him rotten. Well, no way was she going to be one of them. He'd better have a good reason for being late, other than just to rile her, which she wouldn't put past him for a minute.

"Sorry I'm late," he said, mumbling the apology in the manner of someone unused to making one.

"Where were you?" Amanda demanded impatiently. She could have bitten her tongue. It was none of her business where he was.

He told her as much when he grinned widely and said, "Helping a little old lady across the street."

Helping a sweet young thing up off the sheet was probably more like it, Amanda thought, getting into the car.

Kyle closed her door and went around to the driver's side.

"I'm not getting in until you make nice and stop frowning," he said, dangling his car keys in his fingers.

"Will you get in the car," she said humorlessly.

"Yes," he answered, and stood where he was.

She checked her watch nervously. It was five o'clock.

"What time does the movie start?" she asked.

"Five-thirty," he answered, swinging his keys.

"How long does it take to get to the cinema complex?" she asked.

"A half hour," he answered with a bad-boy grin.

"Okay, I'm smiling, see. . . ." she said, flashing him a toothpaste-ad smile. "Now will you get in so we can go?"

He got in.

They weren't on the road five minutes when he pulled into a dry cleaner's.

"What are you doing?" she demanded, a look of complete disbelief registering on her face.

"Picking up my dry cleaning," he answered cheerfully.

"Your dry cleaning!" she yelled.

He threw up his hands in defense. "Look, I have to do it now, okay? They close at six. Besides, it will only take a sec," he promised as he got out of the car.

He'd left his keys in the car when he went inside the dry cleaner's. If she'd known where the cinema was, she'd have driven off and left him there. But she didn't, so she sat in the car and fumed.

She calmed down when she saw him come back out a few seconds later, his dry cleaning in hand, true to his word.

Just as he was walking to the car, a convertible squealed into the parking lot and pulled up alongside Kyle's Mustang.

Amanda turned to see two teenage girls, with bangs waved high and stiffened to perfection, get out of the convertible. One of them whispered excitedly to the other, "I told you it was him."

Amanda's hands clenched into fists when she heard the teenager squeal, "Kyle...Kyle Fox! Is it really you?" as he walked toward the Mustang and Amanda.

He stopped, flipped up his sunglasses and smiled.

The two girls melted into a fit of self-conscious giggles.

"Why hello, girls. Are you fans of *Theater Talk*?" he asked, as if he had all the time in the world.

"We wouldn't miss it," they chorused. "Could we have your autograph?"

Amanda's blood began to boil. "Good idea, girls, because it's going to be real valuable, real soon...

because he's going to be real dead, real soon, and I'm going to enjoy every minute of wringing his gorgeous neck," she muttered under her breath as she sat waiting in the car.

Of course, they didn't have paper on them, and he had to wait while they scrounged some from inside the dry cleaner's. He'd refused to sign their T-shirts with the girls inside them, which surprised Amanda.

Five more precious minutes were wasted until Kyle made it back to the car.

"Fan's," he said with a shake of his head, as if it were their fault instead of his that they were late.

"You may as well take me back to the motel," Amanda said.

"Love to," Kyle said, turning to her and wiggling his eyebrows lasciviously. "But work calls and we've got a movie to review."

Amanda groaned. He was impossible. "You know what I meant," she said. "I'm not walking into the movie after it's already started."

"Don't worry, I'll get you there. I know a shortcut," he said. Like a pilot, he slid his sunglasses down from his head as if they were goggles and tossed the ends of his white silk scarf to one side as he put the car in gear.

Amanda sighed and slumped in her seat. The word "shortcut" was not music to her ears. It didn't take much imagination to visualize the pitfalls of the word, and Amanda had a surplus of imagination.

But true to his word, Kyle pulled into the parking lot of the cinema complex a short time later.

"I don't believe it," she said, opening her eyes. She'd kept them squeezed shut as he'd raced through the streets like a New York cab driver.

Kyle looked at her in amusement. "What? That you're still in one piece or that I got you here on time?"

"Either," Amanda answered, checking her watch. It was 5:25. "You really did get us here on time."

"I said I would, didn't I?" Kyle replied as they got out of the car. He came around to join her and chucked her beneath her chin. "You gotta learn to trust me, sweetheart."

Her muttered reply made him laugh.

When they got inside the mall, Amanda groaned. There was a long line at the ticket counter. The death-defying trip had been for nothing. They were going to have to go to a later show, anyway.

Kyle turned Amanda's chin toward him to get her attention, reached into the pocket of his bomber jacket, pulled out two theater tickets and flashed them in front of her eyes.

"But how . . . ?" she asked.

Kyle waggled his finger at her and grinned. "Uh-uh. What'd I tell you about learning to trust me? Now, I promised Noah I'd pick up some peppermints for him. There's a special kind he likes at a store a few doors down the mall. Here, you hold the tickets and wait right here, and I'll be back in just a sec."

"But . . ." she began objecting, looking down at her watch.

Kyle winked and mouthed the words "Trust me" as he took off at a half run down the mall.

Amanda looked around as she waited impatiently. The mall was new to her, yet familiar. It followed the general pattern of newer shopping malls, with the lower level being occupied by a cinema complex, a food court and several small boutiques. The mall's developer had used a lot of Art Deco design as its stylistic signature.

She looked at her watch again. The show would start in one minute, and there was no sign of Kyle.

As she waited she had a sudden flash of panic that all her success up to now had been a fluke. Where was the exit?

No. She was being ridiculous. It was her concentration she was really worried about. Two new elements had been added to her way of working: she was going to be viewing the movie with an audience—and with Kyle. She wasn't certain which would affect her concentration most, but she could hazard a guess.

Amanda saw that the line at the ticket counter had dwindled to nothing, and she glanced at her watch. It was 5:40. The show had already started. So much for trusting Kyle Fox, she thought, then turned at the sound of running footsteps.

It was him.

She glared at him.

He threw up his hands. "The register tape ran out. What could I do?" he said, shoving the bag of peppermints in his jacket pocket and taking her arm.

"Wait," Amanda said, pulling away from him as he headed them toward the ticket taker. "We can't go in there now."

"Excuse me?" Kyle asked incredulously.

"We can't go in there now," Amanda repeated, biting her bottom lip.

"We can't?" Kyle turned to her, hand on hip. "Are you going to tell me why, or do I have to guess?"

"The feature's already started," Amanda explained, speaking to him slowly, as if he were of questionable intelligence.

"I know that. But, it's only been on for—" he reached for her wrist and checked her watch "—ten minutes at the most. Five minutes of that is previews. I don't make a practice of it, but missing five minutes isn't going to make or break the film. I've missed more than that before and had no trouble reviewing the movie."

She stood staring at him, refusing to give in—either to his argument or the delicious tingle his touch had elicited.

"Do you realize how ridiculously stubborn you're being?" Kyle forced the words through clenched teeth, his demeanor all heated frustration and dark blond machismo.

Amanda stood firm against it's admitted effect. "I am not being ridiculous." Now he had her clenching her teeth.

"A-man-da . . . !"

People were giving them curious glances, but she held her ground. Moviegoers in the smaller market she'd worked in had spent their hard-earned money based on her judgments. They deserved a professional review, and that meant watching the movie from opening to closing credits. "Kyle, it's just not proper," she objected finally.

"Hell, neither am I, but you're just going to have to get used to it."

"And you're going to have to get used to showing up on time," she countered.

He ignored her dig and got down to the problem at hand. Precious minutes were wasting, and he didn't want to go in halfway through the film. "Look," he said, "I assure you moviegoers are late sometimes, too. That doesn't prevent them from going in after the feature's started."

"I don't care. I'm not."

He surveyed her tweed trousers, white flannel jacket and turtleneck sweater and threw up his arms in disgust. "I don't believe you. Your mind is as locked up and buttoned-down as your clothes."

Amanda ignored his remark about her clothes but couldn't resist making her point. "Don't you scowl at me. If we were reviewing movies the proper way, we'd have advance screenings and you wouldn't have to put up with theater schedules. You could have the movie start when you chose to arrive."

"You can forget that idea. I like a crowd."

"You mean you like an audience," Amanda said, and immediately regretted her words. She hadn't meant to let him provoke her, but he seemed to do it as he did everything else . . . effortlessly. Damn him.

Still, having gotten her shot in, she was going to have to make nice. She was, after all, the new kid on the block. If she wanted their on-air partnership to be a success, she needed Kyle's cooperation.

"We can see the next showing," Amanda suggested reasonably.

"I can't, I've got a date," he lied. "Now are you coming?"

He had a date. Amanda was suddenly tired and conceded against her better judgment. "Oh, all right. I wouldn't want you to cancel something important, like a date, over me."

Kyle's victory grin appeared suddenly, then disappeared just as suddenly when he saw Amanda's reaction to it.

He took the tickets from her, handed them to the ticket taker, then ushered her inside the dark and crowded theater. There wasn't much choice in seating. He found two seats in the back row and stood aside to let her in first, taking the aisle seat to accommodate his long legs.

The previews were over, the opening credits were over, and the movie was well under way. Amanda was trying to make the best of the situation. A situation that had quickly gone from bad to worse. Kyle's physical presence in the dark, intimate theater was having a decided effect on her. Ignoring that effect wasn't going to be the piece of cake she'd tried to convince herself it would be.

She couldn't quite see him sitting there beside her; her eyes were still making the adjustment from light to dark, but every nerve in her body assured her he was there. The seats were small and close together in the shoe-box-size theater. Kyle's mossy after-shave was potent at such close range, stimulating her senses and enhancing her disturbing feelings of arousal as they sat with their arms touching from shoulder to elbow.

She tried to concentrate on the screen, but the dangerous romantic visions going on inside her head distracted her and caused her to jump nervously when Kyle relaxed his leg against hers.

The tantalizing aroma of fresh popcorn wafted in from the lobby. Kyle's stomach growled it's acknowledgment.

Whispering to Amanda that he'd be right back, Kyle headed for the concession stand. When he returned a few minutes later, he was carrying a large container of hot, buttered popcorn that smelled heavenly and a couple of cold drinks.

"Fighting whets my appetite," he whispered, handing over her drink. "Besides, it's a sacrilege to watch a movie without eating popcorn." Sliding into his seat, he nestled the container of popcorn between his thighs and leaned close to her ear, whispering, "Help yourself to a handful whenever you want."

She knew he was getting back at her for arguing with him. Well, there was no way she was reaching into his lap for anything. But she did. There was something about the smell of fresh popped popcorn she'd never been able to resist. But she wasn't about to look over at him and see the satisfied smile she was sure had taken up residence on his lips.

She ignored him as she reached for the warm popcorn, building up a lazy rhythm: hand to mouth, hand to mouth. Occasionally, their slippery hands would collide in sensual contact as their fingers scrunched into the container. If it seemed to happen more frequently as time passed, it was surely just coincidence.

Amanda's hand became smeary with butter and salt, and she raised it helplessly, at a loss about how to clean it. Kyle had thought of everything but napkins.

"Why don't you just lick it?" Kyle leaned in to whisper.

His timing and delivery was flawless. Oh, he was bad.

It was delicious torture feeling his eyes on her as she tentatively slipped her finger into her mouth. She squirmed under his gaze, feeling as if he were watching something much more intimate. When he moved beside her, she jumped involuntarily, then felt foolish. He'd only been reaching for his handkerchief.

She wiped her fingers and mouth with the soft cotton cloth. It smelled faintly of his after shave. He must have slipped it in his pocket right after shaving. She dropped the handkerchief in her lap and reached for another handful of popcorn, beginning her lazy hand to mouth, hand to mouth rhythm again, becoming absorbed in the movie, until she no longer bothered to look when she extended her hand. Which was a mistake.

Reaching absently for the last handful of popcorn, she was mortified to find that Kyle had set the empty container on the floor. When her hand touched his crotch, she met obvious evidence that he dressed to the left. He didn't jump at her touch. Instead, he went absolutely still. Why was he somewhat aroused?

She pulled her hand back from the shape of him and muttered her apologies. She wasn't sure, but she thought she heard strangling sounds coming from

Kyle's direction. Well, she wasn't going to look. If he was choking on a popcorn kernel, he would just have to choke.

Finally he made a slurping sound with his drink and seemed to be all right. She sat chewing the ice from the bottom of her drink, trying to pretend she hadn't touched him so intimately. That was hard to do when the very air between them was now redolent with sexuality. They were for all intents and purposes sitting in a darkened movie theater on a Saturday night like a couple of teenagers. Only unlike those teenagers, they weren't climbing all over each other. But they were thinking about it. Or at least she was.

She tried to concentrate on the movie, hoping it would distract her. Wrong.

About halfway through, Kyle stretched and casually put his arm along the back of her seat. Amanda sat tensely, conscious of his arm resting gently against her. She tried not to let it encourage her to lean toward him and rest her head on his shoulder as she wanted to. She was finding the combined scent of his spicy after-shave and the buttered popcorn a powerful aphrodisiac.

The second half of the movie had no chance at competing with the fantasy unfolding in her head.

Kyle cleared his throat when the credits started to roll. The sound brought Amanda back to reality with a start. The movie was over. She was so embarrassed. How could she have made such a stupid blunder? How was she ever going to face him? Maybe he would be a gentleman and let her pretend it had never happened.

As the houselights went on, Kyle leaned close and whispered, his voice as suggestive as a young marine's wink, "I could cancel my date."

He wasn't going to be a gentleman.

Well, he was going to get a lady. Knowing how much he hated prim and proper, Amanda hid her embarrassment behind it. In her best snitty voice, she replied, "If I've turned you on, it was strictly accidental, I can assure you."

Kyle, who had only been teasing . . . well, half teasing, had had enough of her prim and proper for one night.

His response when it came carried a thread of amusement.

"Sort of boggles the mind to imagine what you'd do to turn me on on purpose."

AT TEN O'CLOCK that same evening, all the shops in the mall had closed. The cinema box office was the only place doing any business.

Kyle picked up the ticket the young ticket seller slid toward him.

"Must be a good movie, huh?" the ticket seller asked, remembering Kyle from earlier in the day.

Kyle didn't answer her question. He was in a real bad mood. He was feeling vulnerable and refusing to acknowledge it. Instead, he focused on Amanda Butterworth as the problem. How did one compete with a woman? *Did* one compete with a woman? If he was competitive and aggressive, he would look like a bully.

His evil twin, Lyle, the one he'd invented in childhood to take the blame for all the devilish urges he acted on, had surfaced yesterday outside Noah's office when he'd used his size and anger to intimidate Amanda. She'd been right to call him on it. He was sorry, but he wouldn't let her know he regretted the kiss, even if he had enjoyed it.

He was too afraid of losing.

"Why has Noah taken it into his head to give me a cohost?" he mumbled to himself as he entered the theater.

"I don't want any cohost," he muttered, sitting down in the back of the near-empty room. And he certainly didn't want Amanda Butterworth.

Oh, but he did.

ACROSS TOWN, Amanda paid for a ticket to see the same movie.

This time she saw the movie in it's entirety, from opening to closing credits. And she saw it without distraction.

Unless, of course, you counted her bad mood.

She was annoyed by, yet immensely enjoyed, the erotic thoughts of Kyle that popped into her mind when she wasn't on her guard. They'd begun with the starched white tuxedo shirt she'd imagined unbuttoning upon first meeting him and had gotten progressively more wicked, wilder and wetter.

The plots she constructed in her head to get even with him had grown more diabolical hourly and thus were useless. What she needed was a simple way to unnerve him the way he unbalanced her. There had to be some chink in the bored, smugly amused armor he wore.

Every time she thought about Kyle's amused response to her putdowns, her hand itched to slap his face.

He was the *most* aggravating, conceited, annoying, arrogant . . . handsome, sexy, exciting . . .

3

By Tuesday, Amanda had managed to review three more movies. She had met Kyle for all of them. Ignoring his amused smile, she'd bought her own box of popcorn and sat as far away from him as possible. Noah had said he'd like them to attend the same screenings, but he hadn't said anything about them having to sit together.

Her free time had been taken up with moving into her new apartment, which had once been a carriage house that someone had converted. The living room and galley kitchen made up the first floor and a loft bedroom and bath were upstairs, with French doors leading off the bedroom to a small sunny balcony. Finding the carriage house had been a great stroke of luck, and the hectic activity of moving in had been a perfect antidote to thoughts of Kyle.

Amanda had spent the day dusting and scrubbing her new place, and she was hot, damp and tired. On her way upstairs to the bathroom to wash her hands, she lifted the wild mass of brown hair off her neck and blew a stream of air up to her face to cool off. Catching a glimpse of herself in the mirror on the bathroom door, she smiled.

If he could see her now, Kyle wouldn't think she was so prim and proper. The T-shirt, which was all she had on, barely skimmed the top of her thighs and clung to the curves of her damp skin, making her look positively nubile.

After washing up, she headed downstairs, trailing her hand along the smooth banister she'd cleaned and polished. She looked out the small octagonal window in the kitchen at the acrobatics of a silly gray squirrel trying to get into the bird feeder she'd put up. She smiled with contentment. It was pure bliss to finally have a place of her own. When she'd lived in the same town as her parents, her father had insisted it was foolish for her to waste money renting. So she'd lived at home and saved her money.

She'd used a chunk of her savings to buy the essentials for the carriage house: a brass bed, an antique oak writing desk and chair, a dusty pink contemporary love seat, a glass coffee table and a tall, intricately carved armoire to hold the television and stereo system she'd splurged on.

Though she hadn't bought a lot of furniture, the way she'd placed it in the small rooms gave the carriage house a warm coziness, as well as a spare, modern feel.

The record playing on the stereo ended, and her Whitesnake album dropped to the turntable, the lead singer's raspy voice asking, "Is this love?"

The song made her think of Kyle. No, it wasn't love, but it certainly was lust. And it made her job twice as difficult.

The last *Theater Talk* with Kyle alone was due to start. She flipped on the television and made her way back to the kitchen to fix a salad. By the time she finished tossing the salad ingredients, Kyle's image was flickering on the screen. Breaking off a crusty end of French bread, she picked up her salad and iced tea and carried them to the glass coffee table fronting her squishy, big-pillowed love seat. Tucking her feet beneath her, she settled in to watch *Theater Talk*, delighting in the feel of the soft upholstery on her bare skin.

Remembering her admonition, she steeled herself to resist the undeniable pull of Kyle's charisma.... Little good it did her. The chalk-striped thirties-style suit he was wearing fit him like a dream, making a princely assault on her resolve. His tan made his blue eyes even bluer, and she could almost smell the mossy scent of his after-shave on his clean-shaved jaw. His dark blond hair grazed the English spread collar of his starchy white shirt. A shirt she just knew had French cuffs. Refusing to be susceptible to his admitted charms, she glared at his elegant tie, denying her urge to straighten it, just a little.

As if to thwart her efforts at resistance, his deep, resonant voice floated out from the television and caressed her. It was difficult to stave off the seductive powers of a voice that registered somewhere around 7.8 on her own personal Richter scale. Working opposite him on camera was going to take all of her composure. Frowning, she picked up her salad and speared a bright bit of tomato.

Kyle always opened the program with a commentary on whatever movie tidbit struck his fancy. As he introduced a series of film clips featuring Leslie Masters, Amanda wondered what he was getting at. The actress hadn't appeared in a movie in some time.

"Leslie Masters lights up the screen and reminds us that blondes have more fun," Kyle began, the timbre of his voice low and suggestive, as it had been when he'd proposed dumping his date after Amanda's hand had blundered into his lap at the movie.

Amanda's thinking on the blunder had gone from initial embarrassment to a certain detached enjoyment. At odd moments she found herself delighting in having caught Kyle off guard, however unintentionally. She even found herself lingering over the feel of him. . . .

"Unfortunately for the movies," Kyle went on, "Leslie Masters has moved on to the small screen of television. She put her blonde sizzle into *The Big Corral* several seasons ago, teaming with Jake Ross for some white-hot horsing around on the ranch."

"Oh, I'm sure," Amanda said with a smirk. "Jake Ross is a blast furnace all by himself, you idiot," she muttered to Kyle's image on the television screen, enjoying herself immensely. Having had parents who'd barely noticed her existence, she'd long ago fallen into the habit of entertaining herself.

But the man didn't know when to quit. Now he was rambling on about Leslie Master's current television series.

"Leslie's elbowing her way through the popular Friday-night series *Baker's Place*. It's a shame the only place you can find a sexy, feisty blonde like the ones who lit up the movie screens in the romantic comedies of the thirties and forties is on television. I only wish Miss Masters would do a movie now and then."

Kyle began his closing for the segment with a twinkle in his baby blues. "While there is much that is charming and entertaining on television . . ."

"Cute, Kyle, cute," Amanda sputtered, carrying on her one-sided conversation with his image. The man really had no modesty.

" . . . sitting in a well-lighted living room watching television just isn't the same as sitting in a darkened theater watching a movie—" his voice lowered to a lazy, naughty tease "—sharing the fantasy."

Amanda sat up and took notice.

Why hadn't she thought of it before? It had been right in front of her nose all along. He was a movie reviewer, like herself, so it followed that fantasy would be his weakness.

She smiled a cat-in-the-cream smile.

She had him.

And the great part was, he had been the one to give her the ammunition for her to get even.

Her mind began to plot. She could feel the adrenaline starting to pump through her system and wondered if this was how men always felt at the challenge of seduction.

Flipping off the television, she crossed to the oak writing desk and lifted several sheets of pale pink stationery and a fountain pen from the center drawer and carried them upstairs to the bathroom.

She turned on the taps and began filling the tub with warm water. Then, unwrapping the new bar of scented soap that smelled like fresh rain, she shed her T-shirt and slipped into the inviting, warm water for a long, decadent soak.

She was going to boggle Kyle Fox's mind. He was about to be turned on *on purpose*. Her anticipatory smile was positively wicked as she reached for the pen and paper.

Kyle Fox didn't stand a Yuppie's chance in a redneck bar.

THE TOP WAS OFF Kyle's black Corvette, and the night air felt oddly warm for early March. It looked as if they were in for a couple of days of warm weather. As he sped along the highway, Amanda's image teased his mind. Truth be told, she'd been on his mind more often than not since he'd met her.

He couldn't figure out why, because she annoyed the hell out of him. He hated prim and proper.

It couldn't be her personality that intrigued him. When she wasn't being prickly, she was just too damned nice. It was the only four-letter word that offended him. As far as he was concerned, *nice* was short for *repressed*.

He remembered Amanda's blunder into his lap. As he drove, the wind carried his chuckle away into the night. If she'd known he'd been imagining her purposely caressing him there when it had happened, she would have been mortified. Hell, her touch had almost taken the top of his head off.

But he was quite certain Miss Butterworth never had such lascivious thoughts. Damned shame, too. He wanted her to have the same lascivious thoughts about him he was having about her.

He'd like to slide his hand up her long legs, which she kept encased in those virgin pastel hose, on up under her prim and proper long skirt. As he pulled into the parking space in front of his condo, he grew hard just envisioning it.

He hadn't wanted to like her so much. She probably thought he was a real jerk. It was just that she pushed his buttons when she got frosty on him.

Frustrated, he fumbled with his keys and finally managed to unlock his front door. The scent of a woman's perfume lingering in the air confronted him immediately. He wrinkled his brow in puzzlement. Where in the hell had that come from? He'd never brought a woman to his condo. The few times he'd gotten that involved, he'd preferred going to their place. That way he could leave before things got too domestic.

Showing his true emotions was a bit of a sticky wicket for him. He hid his feelings behind a glib facade women rarely, if ever, got past. Self-disclosure wasn't something he indulged in. His friendships tended to be more on the social side than intimate. The perfume was definitely out of place and therefore disturbing.

Where was it coming from?

Glancing around, his eyes finally lit on a pale pink envelope, addressed to him in a feminine slant, lying on the quarry tile floor of his entranceway. As he bent to pick it up, the source of the perfume lingering in the air became readily apparent. Studying the envelope, he jammed one hand on his hip.

Failing to recognize the handwriting, he carried the envelope to the kitchen with him and laid it on the white Formica countertop. It took him a few minutes to remember where he'd hidden his favorite chocolate chip cookies from himself.

After digging through his pantry, he located the Crock-Pot he'd stashed them in and tore open the package, knowing the binge was going to mean extra sit-ups. It was worth it, he decided when he bit into the rich, gooey cookie. Picking up the curious pink envelope again, he studied it pensively. There was nothing subtle about the scent of the perfume. It's musky, sensual fragrance meant serious business . . . man/woman business.

Should he open it? he wondered, rubbing the cleft in his chin with his long forefinger. He frowned. How had a fan gotten his address? His fan mail usually stacked up unopened at the station, until Noah had Toby package and deliver it to Kyle's condo.

Toby. Kyle grinned, realizing the answer. Toby was no match for a pleading female voice, especially in person, when it was accompanied by long, batting eyelashes. Sometimes he thought Toby worked harder than he did at maintaining his reputation as a ladies' man.

As he held it, trying to make up his mind, the masculinity of his tan hand contrasted with the small, pretty envelope. There was no postmark, so someone had gone to a lot of trouble to hand deliver it and slip it through the mail slot in his door.

Aw, hell, he decided, what could it hurt? After opening the refrigerator to get a cold glass of milk to go with the chocolate chip cookies, he ripped open the envelope before he could think better of it.

As his blue eyes scanned the first few lines, he realized it wasn't an ordinary fan letter. Not ordinary at all. . . .

Kyle,

Your show Tuesday night made it quite clear that blondes are your preference.

I'm not blond, Kyle. But perhaps you'd like me.

Do you like sunny beaches? I do. I'm going for a swim. Do you like my swimsuit? I thought you might. It's strapless, but I don't have any trouble keeping it up, do I, Kyle?

See how high the legs are cut on the curve of my hips . . . leaving only a narrow swath of hot-pink material to slide between my thighs like a man's hand.

Maybe your hand, Kyle?

Feel the heat of the sun's rays beating down. . . . I'll need to use suntan oil. One can't be too careful with soft, tender skin. Don't you want to slick the oil onto my bare skin and smooth your hands over my curves?

That's right. Drizzle oil on my shoulders and down my arms. Pay no attention to the drop of oil that just slithered between my breasts. Concentrate instead on my shoulders. Rub your thumbs slowly along the hollows of my neck. Run your hands leisurely down my arms. I can feel the tremble of your touch, the hot whisper of your breath on my neck. Kyle, you've moved in much too close.

What's that you said? Well, I am tempted to let you do my legs . . . maybe next time. But you can watch. See, I'm putting a little pool of suntan oil in the palm of my hand. Now I'm sliding my hands over my ankles. See the slender gold anklet I wear. Always. My hands are slippery as they smooth up my calves and over my knees. Did you know the backs of my knees are ticklish?

Next my thighs. . . .

Kyle! Give me back the suntan oil. What do you think you're doing . . . soooo well. Oh Kyle! Please. . . .

And Kyle, I swim naked. Do you have any idea how sensuous it feels to have water lapping over every bare inch of you, caressing your skin like a lover's tongue . . . ?

Sleep well, Kyle. . . .

Kyle stood staring at the letter written on pink stationery. How could he be so hot and so cold at the same time? It was then he realized he was standing in front of the open refrigerator with his hand on a carton of cold milk. He'd been standing there in a trance the whole time he'd read the letter. Picking up the carton of milk, he took a large swallow, then set it back in the refrigerator. He finished the last of his chocolate chip cookies and laughed out loud.

Whoever had written the letter had had a great time writing her outrageous fantasy . . . but not half as much fun as he'd had reading it.

He opened the cabinet door beneath the sink to toss the audacious letter into the trash, then changed his mind. His curiosity, among other things, was aroused. He'd like to meet up with the lady who'd written it. If she was anything like the fantasy, she was too good to be true . . . or too bad to be true.

He headed toward his living room, the letter still in his hand. His living room walls were decorated with movie posters, but not old ones. Like everything else in his condo, the posters were up-to-the-minute and on the cutting edge of what was happening. Crossing to his black-lacquered desk, he slipped the letter into the shallow center drawer, and went to take a quick shower.

Ten minutes later, he lay naked across his futon bed, willing himself to sleep. But he didn't.

Instead, he tossed and turned restlessly. He kept seeing the woman described in the fantasy, walking toward him in her incredible hot-pink swimsuit.

Smiling an invitation, she offered him a flask of suntan oil . . . and her very nubile body. And then she was peeling off the swimsuit, arcing into the water. She swam out, turned, then floated toward him on her back and drove him right out of the bed.

As he grabbed his swim trunks from a bottom drawer, he muttered a colorful curse. Pulling them on, he headed for the condo's heated outdoor pool—never mind that it was after midnight. When he got to the pool, he remembered the last line of the fantasy in the letter and discarded his swim trunks.

His final thought before he emptied his mind and sliced through the moonlit water for some serious swimming was that whoever had written the letter was right. The water's lap was silky and sensual against his naked body . . . a lover's caress.

AMANDA WAS DISTRAUGHT. The taping wasn't going well.

Directly across from her sat the person responsible. At the moment, they were waiting for a lighting technician to make an adjustment, and Kyle was giving her that "Who, me?" look of a new puppy who'd just soiled the carpet.

And the worst of it was that he looked just as cute as a new puppy. No. The worst of it was that he knew he looked cute. Today he was wearing—along with his pretense of innocence—a navy flannel one-button suit, a blue-and-white striped cotton shirt, with the French cuffs she'd suspected, red suspenders, a polka-dot silk tie and sexy Italian shoes.

She hadn't known what to expect when they began taping, but Kyle had put her at ease by being polite and listening attentively. After each of her reviews, he'd followed with one of his own.

Following the third one, she'd begun to get nervous. He'd been charming and entertaining, as usual, not letting it show that having a cohost bothered him. He'd also agreed with every one of her reviews. She should have been suspicious at Kyle's offer to let her go first.

It couldn't be coincidence, she was certain. He was doing it on purpose. He knew good and well that without disagreement there would be no controversy. And without controversy, there was no reason to add her to the show. He was shrewdly undermining her debut, letting her know the show belonged to him and he didn't have any intention of sharing it with her.

No wonder he hadn't written a script to consult, as she had. He was winging it. And doing a hell of a good job of shutting her out, Amanda grudgingly admitted to herself. Oh, he was good, all right. But she'd fought hard for her success, and she wasn't going to give up without giving Kyle a battle.

She was going to have to do something—any-thing—to get him going, to get him to disagree with her. It shouldn't be hard. Think. She had to think. He disagreed with her all the time ... about everything.

The lighting technician finished his task, and the taping resumed.

"And so we come to the last movie Miss Butterworth and I will be reviewing today," Kyle informed the camera with a satisfied smile Amanda longed to wipe off his face. "Miss Butterworth...."

"Why don't you go first this time, Mr. Fox?" she said sweetly, foiling his system of sabotaging her reviews.

Kyle was caught off balance by her maneuver, but only momentarily. His smile should have warned her he'd made a quick recovery.

"This one is easy, isn't it?" he began.

Amanda frowned. The movie was one of those dreadful macho vehicles Kyle regularly recommended for their entertainment value. After seeing this one with him, she remembered recommending he not pick any more films to review that were—how had she put it?— oh yeah, "full of car chases, bullets and babes." There was no way they could agree on this film.

"This film is slick and fast, without a memorable plot," he began, "perhaps without even a discernible plot."

Amanda's response was stunned astonishment.

Kyle looked over at her, his devious blue eyes twinkling with mischief. His smile was disarming, but his next line was loaded. "There is however, plenty of action, with car chases, bullets and babes galore. Don't you agree, Miss Butterworth?"

Damn him. He'd taken the words right out of her mouth. Except when he said them, they sounded like a recommendation.

Kyle waited for her to gather her wits, his smug smile saying he knew she was too proper to change her review and play dirty.

Amanda crossed her legs and the lights caught the gold chain on her slender ankle. "I must admit I'm amazed that once again we agree, Mr. Fox. It's a situation I can't imagine continuing."

Glancing at Kyle, Amanda's mood swung from total frustration to mounting amusement. Kyle's attention had leaped to her anklet, his gaze riveting on the slender gold chain. His eyes narrowed as he continued to stare. She knew where his mind had traveled. . . .

Knowing she was grasping at straws, she nevertheless seized the opportunity and took her best available shot.

"It's true we do agree it was an action film on the surface, but I believe you missed the underlying point the director was trying to make about a common problem in relationships. That is that men don't listen to women when they talk. Don't you agree, Mr. Fox?"

"Huh?"

Amanda enjoyed letting him hang out to dry a moment. Trying to keep the triumph from her voice and not succeeding, she borrowed one of Kyle's smug smiles and said, "My point, exactly."

The protest she'd expected wasn't long in coming.

"What the hell are you talking about? Wait a minute.... Cut!" Kyle yelled, remembering suddenly that they were still on camera.

He tore at the mike on his shirt and it snagged. The worm had turned and he was no longer smugly in control. He hadn't heard a word Amanda had said since she'd crossed her legs and the light had caught her ankle bracelet. Surely Miss Butter-wouldn't-melt-in-her-mouth couldn't have written him the steamy fantasy. Nah ... that was just wishful thinking on his part.

Off to one side, Noah ran his hand over his bald head and smiled. The taping had gotten off to an unexpectedly tame start, but the finish was perfect. Kyle's faux pas ought to stimulate some lively dinner table conversations between couples.

As Amanda left the set, she smiled her first smile since the taping had begun. No matter how much Kyle protested, Noah insisted Kyle's dumbfounded "Huh?" be the closing for the segment.

When it came to blunders, they were even. Still, she couldn't help feeling ahead. Her blunder had been in the dark, unseen by anyone. His had been on tape, to be seen by everyone.

Kyle was still on the set. Toby was helping him unsnag his microphone.

"What kind of swimsuit do you think Miss Butterworth wears?" he asked the young intern.

"Miss Butterworth ... ?"

"Never mind," Kyle said as he watched Amanda walk away in her caramel-colored mock-turtleneck sweater, narrow, ankle-length, tobacco-colored suede skirt and proper alligator pumps. Her brown hair was pulled back in a chignon so tight her toenails probably hurt.

He must be losing his mind.

Amanda was as likely to shed her inhibitions as he was to run for political office.

4

THE DEEJAY WAS SPINNING her favorite song on the radio, but Amanda didn't notice. Nor had she noticed the hints of early spring in the air or the pretty scenery all around her as she drove to meet Kyle at the cinema complex in the mall. Her mind kept drifting back to Friday's taping of *Theater Talk*.

Stopping for a red light, she continued to mull over Kyle's behavior. She still had trouble believing he'd pulled such a dirty trick. It had been a cheap shot, agreeing with every one of her reviews. One she wouldn't have thought him capable of.

What had prompted his low-down, underhanded behavior? she wondered. Did she threaten him that much? Could it be possible he wasn't really as self-assured as he came across? It was true she didn't actually know much about Kyle Fox, other than his reputation. She supposed a reputation based on sex appeal could leave one feeling uncertain about their professional ability.

Her confidence in her professional ability was built on hard work. She knew her movie history cold. And her fans had confirmed her judgment, agreeing with her reviews of movies nine times out of ten.

Perhaps she was conning herself, looking for a reason to believe Kyle was better than he was because she was so attracted to him.

So he was gorgeous. She hadn't exactly fallen off the turnip truck when she'd arrived at KCNX. She'd seen gorgeous guys before, had even dated her share.

The bottom line was that none of them, other than the actors up on the screen in a darkened movie theater—had ever stirred the intimate feelings and fantasies that thoughts of Kyle conjured.

He was a living, breathing man, and as her co-worker, as untouchable as the make-believe characters on screen. She was going to have to learn to control her sultry thoughts of him. Certainly one of them thinking he was God's gift to women was more than enough.

Waiting for the light to change to green, her hands drummed nervously against the wheel. Today would be their first viewing of a film since Kyle had pulled his stunt of agreeing with all her reviews. Why did she have to feel all melted bones in the presence of someone who disdained her?

The light changed to green, and she turned into the shopping center parking lot.

At least there were limits to what she'd do in the name of competition, though she'd be foolish not to take advantage of any good luck, breaks or opportunities that came her way.

Breaks like Kyle's fascination with her anklet when they were on camera. It had led to his faux pas, giving her the opportunity to make something of a comeback in her goal of creating a controversial show. If Noah's response was any indication, she'd salvaged the taping from being a total flop, at least.

A tiny smile touched her lips as she recalled how the taping had ended. She wondered what kind of response Kyle's blundered "Huh?" would elicit from *Theater Talk*'s audience when it was shown this week. With any luck at all, it would create the kind of controversy that would increase *Theater Talk*'s audience, thereby building the odds in her favor when it came to her continuing with the show.

As she strode inside the mall, she checked her watch and determined she was ahead of schedule. Not only would she have time to drop off her anklet at the jeweler's for repair, but there would be time to do some browsing before she had to meet Kyle. Maybe she could walk off some of her jitters. She had a feeling Kyle wasn't going to be pleased to see her, not that he ever was.

The shopping center was fairly empty. It was the time of day when shoppers abandoned the malls to get home before their children returned on the school bus. Amanda felt more comfortable without the crowds. The bump and shuffle of crowded malls still unnerved her a little. She was used to space to maneuver in. Though she loved the big city's advantages, she hadn't yet made the conversion to big-city dweller.

At the jeweler's she dropped off the anklet she'd broken pulling on her boots. It was the only anklet she owned. She'd have to be more careful of the delicate chain in the future, noting that the price of gold soldering had inched up again.

Leaving the jeweler's with a good half hour to kill, she stopped to browse at the little perfumery jutting out into the mall walkway. Perfumes were a particular weakness of hers.

As Amanda browsed, a pretty salesgirl wearing too much makeup studied her. Amanda's hair was sleeked back in a ponytail clasped in a banana comb. Her raspberry lip gloss was her only discernible makeup. The salesgirl was about to suggest a pure, clean-scented cologne when Amanda picked up a small, smooth amber bottle.

She recognized it from the exquisitely sensual print ads on the glossy pages of fashion magazines. The ads had intrigued her so, she'd sent for a sample vial of the perfume, using an order blank from a special promotion in the magazine. It had been that sample she'd sprinkled over the fantasy she'd written to Kyle. If she was going to write another fantasy, she would need some more of the same perfume.

She paused briefly to consider. *Was* she going to send him another fantasy?

He deserved one as retribution for the stunt he'd pulled at the taping. She smiled at the name of the perfume in her hand—Pleasure.

"I'll take this," Amanda said, handing the salesgirl the provocative perfume.

"Would you like it in any other form? A bath powder or cream, perhaps?"

"No, that will do," Amanda answered, her eyes sparkling with secret satisfaction. She couldn't actually wear the perfume without giving away the game.

When the sale was completed, Amanda still had a good twenty minutes to kill. She didn't want to face Kyle any sooner than she had to.

Deciding to splurge on a pair of silk stockings, she headed across the mall to the lingerie boutique. The shop's sweet fragrance met her at the door.

"Hi," the young girl behind the counter called as Amanda walked deeper into the boutique.

"Hello," Amanda answered, heading for the display of stockings.

Making her selection, Amanda handed them to the teenager.

"Silk stockings. . . ." The teenager sighed. "My Aunt Zoe says they feel wonderful. She owns this boutique and lets me work here after school. I'm going to major in fashion merchandising."

"It's a lovely shop," Amanda commented, continuing to browse.

"If you like teddies, some really radical ones came in today," the teenager said, pointing to a rack of provocative teddies on the side wall of the tiny boutique.

Since she still had time to kill, Amanda wandered over to the display and in no time at all found a demure white teddy with a touch of wispy lace. There was no one else in the boutique, and the teenager cajoled her into taking it to try on in one of the shuttered dressing rooms that lined the back wall.

Amanda hadn't needed much encouragement and laughingly added a satiny black camisole and tap pants on her way. Inside the dressing room, she hung the lingerie on the white china hook above a little blue velvet chair. When she slipped out of her clothes and boots, she studied her reflection in the mirror. Her skin was a peachy-cream color unkissed by the sun, and her curves were sleek.

Smiling at the folly of the demure white teddy, she stepped into it. Her image in the mirror pleased her. She looked . . . well, sexy.

Was it time she stopped concentrating on her career so intently that she obliterated the trappings of femininity? she wondered. Time she took some chances and stopped playing safe?

What would Kyle think about the scrap of nothing she was wearing, she mused, trying to study her reflection with his eyes.

She was just pulling up the ribbon strap that had slipped off her shoulder when she heard a deep male voice, the very sound of it causing her nipples to pebble against the smooth silk in response.

"I wonder if you could assist me, miss? I've been given strict instructions that I'm to purchase a chemise, yet I'm not certain I know what one is, exactly."

Amanda's consciousness recognized Kyle Fox's voice just seconds after her body did, and she froze, staring at her sensual image in the mirrored dressing room. A blush of embarrassment stained her cheeks. Irrationally, she felt he could see her standing there, wearing the provocative wisp of nothing, her body aroused merely by the sound of his voice. She peered cautiously through the slats in the dressing room door.

"Ah . . . ah . . ." the teenager stuttered. "Ah . . . right. We have some over here on this rack," she finally managed, recovering her composure somewhat. The time of day she worked didn't usually bring in men. Though

Kyle's sexual charisma would have left her tongue-tied in any situation.

Kyle nodded and followed the teenager to the rack she indicated, where she selected a chemise trimmed in cameo lace and offered it for his inspection.

"Do you have the same thing in white?" Kyle asked, satisfied with the style.

"Uh . . . do you know . . . uh . . . the size?"

Kyle squinted a minute and thought. "A small ought to do it, I think."

The teenager disappeared to check the stockroom in the back of the boutique.

Amanda's hand flew to her lips and her body stiffened in apprehension when Kyle turned and walked directly toward her dressing room. She stopped breathing until she realized he wasn't going to fling open the shuttered door and expose her. It had only been her imagination running amuck.

She exhaled with relief when she saw him stop a few feet from her to examine a white teddy, the same style she had on. His hand reached to slide the material between his fingertips, and she turned away, feeling as if he were touching her somehow. She slipped the white teddy she'd tried on from her body and tossed it onto the little velvet chair.

The sudden movement in the quiet, empty boutique caught Kyle's attention. His eyes lingered with naughty indulgence on the delicate ankles and prettily arched feet visible beneath the shuttered dressing room door. The nails on the toes of the slender feet were painted a pastel shade that blushed sweetly against the apricot carpet of the boutique. Kyle's tongue roamed the inside of his cheek as he savored graceful hands, their long nails painted the same pastel shade, slipping black satin tap pants up over bare feet and sleek calves. A quiet sigh escaped his lips as his mind visualized the scene behind the door.

The sound caused Amanda to check on his whereabouts nervously. She peeked out the shuttered door and saw him studying an outrageously sexy, red merry widow on display close by. She watched as he fingered the passionate touches of lace along it's demi cups and above the snappy garters. The matching bikini panty was nothing more than a playful bit of lace on satin. Savage, risqué thoughts glittered in her eyes.

"I found one. You were lucky. It's the last one we have in that size in white," the teenage salesgirl called, returning from the back of the boutique. "Is it a gift? Do you want me to wrap it for you?"

The teenager's return had interrupted the intensely erotic moment Kyle and Amanda had shared... separately. Amanda looked down at her palms sheltering her naked breasts. A rosy flush suffused her skin when she realized her fingers were squeezing them.

Kyle had turned from the merry widow to answer, "Yeah, that'd be great. I'm all thumbs when it comes to wrapping things."

The air conditioning kicked on in the boutique, and the vent above Amanda blew cool air over her flushed body.

"I'll be right with you when I finish with this customer," the teenager called out to her cheerfully.

Amanda cringed, feeling guilty and exposed.

Kyle slid his charge card back into his wallet after signing the carboned slip. When the teenager had his package ready, he took the gaily wrapped box from her, his peripheral vision catching a glimpse of black satin falling against the apricot carpet of the dressing room. A softly erotic image of the woman who'd been trying on that bit of black sin stole into his mind.

He was smiling his secret thoughts as he entered the card shop in search of a birthday card for his little sister to go with the present he'd just bought to mail her.

AMANDA HURRIED TOWARD the escalator after stashing her purchases in the trunk of her car. She'd been so flustered she'd bought both the demure white teddy and the racy black camisole with its matching tap pants. The subtle eroticism of the boutique and the feelings Kyle's presence had stirred had threatened her sense of control.

He wasn't waiting for her outside the cinema as she'd expected. Figuring he'd already gone inside since she was running late, she got her ticket at the box office and entered the cinema lobby.

Kyle was leaning against a wall, his hand resting on his hip, the package from the lingerie boutique set at his feet. He and the package were a sexy combination, inviting all kinds of fantasies in her mind.

When he caught her eye, he looked down at his watch pointedly, then back up at her. "Did you just get here?" he demanded in mock-outrage, getting back at her for her tirade over his tardiness at the first film they'd previewed together.

"Uh . . . yes," she lied.

"Trying to avoid me so you won't have to explain that little stunt you pulled on me at the taping?" he asked, baiting her.

"Me!"

"Yes, you." He raked his hard eyes over her. "You know perfectly well you set me up real good."

"Did I?" Amanda asked blithely. Trying to make a stab at recovering her composure, she moved to the concession stand to get her popcorn and soda.

" 'Did I?' " Kyle mocked in a falsetto, picking up the package at his feet and following her. "Come on, you don't really expect me to believe you're as innocent as you act. Hell, nobody's *that* damn innocent."

Better to get away from that line of thought, Amanda decided, remembering the fantasy she'd sent him. "And I suppose you didn't plan to ambush me with all those ridiculous reviews you did, agreeing with me at every turn?"

"Don't get righteous on me, lady. You're the one who invaded my turf. I wouldn't be much of a man if I took it lying down on my back, would I?" His smile had double entendre written all over it.

Amanda ignored the double entendre. "Look, I'm not trying to take anything away from you. I only want to make things better. If we share—"

"Yeah, that's what the whites told the Indians."

"Why can't—"

"Look, we'll argue later. The movie's going to start, and you know what a fuss you make over being late," he said, steering her and her popcorn toward the theater showing the feature they were to review.

"What about your popcorn? Aren't you having any?"

"You're the one who's so big on sharing...so I'll have some of yours," he answered, sliding into the seat beside her. He had her, but not quite yet where he wanted her.

KYLE SLID INTO his black Corvette, anxious to get home. The speech he'd given at the college on new directors had gone well, but the question-and-answer period had seemed to last forever. He'd had trouble concentrating on the questions and hadn't done his reputation as an astute movie critic much good. It was all Amanda's fault. Everyone he met wanted to know all about his new partner and what had happened on *Theater Talk*. The tape he and Amanda had done together had been shown Tuesday night. They were due to tape next Tuesday's show tomorrow night.

It was a warm, muggy evening, and the breeze created by the speeding Corvette did little more than fan hot air at him. He'd taken off his unstructured navy jacket and laid it on the empty passenger seat. His narrow leather tie, which had nearly strangled him, was lying across his jacket. As he drove he rolled up the sleeves of his shirt. At least the gray pleated pants he wore were lightweight and cool. He could put the top on and turn on the air conditioner, but he liked to feel the wind rushing against his skin.

He stopped at the drive-through window of a restaurant along the way and picked up some roasted chicken. He'd been busy and had forgotten to eat all day. During the rest of the drive home, he listened to a tape he'd mixed himself. The first song was "Pink Cadillac." It was great driving with the top down to that sort of song. It ended and Aretha Franklin started up "Who's Zoomin' Who?" Yeah, he wondered. Who *was* zooming who?

He'd sat with Amanda reviewing a feature Monday night. It hadn't worked. He'd wound up once again having to preview the movie over. When he was that close to her, whatever was on the screen couldn't compete. The rest of the week, she hadn't had to choose a seat far away from him at the previews. He'd taken care of avoiding sitting next to her. Could she really be as innocent of her effect on him as she let on?

The aroma of the roasted chicken wafted from the take-out package, and his stomach told him to open the package and munch. But he was much too fastidious a person to eat in the car.

When he pulled up in front of his condo, he wondered if there would be a pink envelope waiting for him. If he was honest, he had to admit that was the reason he was in such a hurry to get home. That and the roasted chicken. Any way you looked at it, he was hungry. He'd been surprised to find he was more than a little disappointed there hadn't been a follow-up by the fan who'd written him the fantasy letter.

A few minutes later he was opening his door and his nostrils were being assaulted with the sexy perfume he remembered. A smile wreathed his face as he glanced down at the quarry tile entranceway, anticipating a pink envelope lying in wait. What the . . . ? His smile wilted. There was no envelope.

Where was the perfume coming from? Had the fan gotten a key somehow? Was she here waiting for him? He walked through his living room and on to the kitchen. Setting the package of roasted chicken down on the counter, he looked around him and followed his nose. The smell was so slight in the kitchen as to be nonexistent, but the closer he got to the front door, the stronger the scent became. And then he saw the pink from the corner of his eye. The envelope had gotten caught on the mail slot's flap. He reached for it with a sigh of relief.

Letter in hand, he went back to his chicken and un-packaged it, setting everything on a plate. Taking a wine cooler from the refrigerator, he grabbed the plate and envelope and headed for the little balcony off his bedroom, where he had a small white metal bistro set. He set the food on the table and went back in his bed-room to take off his clothes. He wanted to sit on the balcony naked but slipped on a pair of khaki shorts in deference to propriety.

The pink envelope rested against the umbrella pole of the bistro table. The light from the bedroom spilled out onto the balcony, enabling him to study it as he ate. He didn't recognize the handwriting other than it matched the original pink envelope from last week.

If this was a plot to arouse his interest, it was work-ing just dandy. But why didn't the person show her-self? Why all the secrecy?

When he finished the last of his chicken dinner, he licked his fingers slowly and leisurely, then pushed the plate away from him. Reaching for the letter, he drained the last of the wine cooler. A wicked smile of antici-pation played on his lips, and a certain gleam flickered in his eyes.

Kyle,

Have you missed me? It's been one whole week. Did you like the letter I sent you?

I'm wearing my black satin camisole for you right now. It feels cool and smooth against my bare skin. Can you imagine it beneath your warm hands?

Did you know you were there when I bought it, Kyle? Think back. Do you remember shopping in the lingerie boutique a few days ago? Remember... there was someone in one of the dressing rooms. I was trying on the black satin camisole while you shopped.

But enough about then, Kyle. . . . I want you to be here with me now. I'm back at the boutique. The shop is empty. The salesgirl has gone. I'm waiting for you in the dressing room. It's just large enough for the two of us, if you don't mind being a little cramped.

You like what I'm wearing, don't you, Kyle? I saw you admiring it on the mannequin. It looks better on a real woman, doesn't it? It's as red as a cherry lollipop. But not nearly so innocent. A merry widow is worn for only one reason—pure, naughty pleasure.

Would you like to slide your hands over the smooth satin where it hugs my curves? Here, let me arch toward you so your hands can span my waist. I love your hands, Kyle. They're so very male. . . .

Do you like the playful garters? See how they leave a little red mark like a love bite when I snap them against my thigh? Notice the contrast of the black stockings against my skin . . . the subtle eroticism where dark stocking leaves off and pale skin begins. Isn't your eye enticed to linger there? Why, Kyle darling, your eyes are deepening to the darkest shade of blue. . . .

This wispy bit of bikini panty feels so sexy. The lace scratches ever so exquisitely low across my abdomen. Would you like to slide this layer of soft romance away?

No, I've got a better idea. Close your eyes, Kyle. Are they closed tightly? Now, give me your hands. You're so warm. . . . Here, slide your hand beneath the panty and see touch me. Yes, I like that. . . .

Oh . . . Kyle! No, you must stop. Really, you must. I hear somebody in the boutique. . . . Quick, you must leave!

Have a nice shower, Kyle . . .

Kyle sat staring at the pale stationery. He'd been in that dressing room with her.

Even to the point of seeing things she hadn't described, like what the back of her body looked like reflected in the mirror as he'd embraced her. He could smell the fragrance of the boutique even now.

Who was this woman?

How had she known he was going to be in the boutique? Was she following him around? No, she'd been in the boutique before he'd entered it. Coincidence. It had to be a coincidence.

Didn't it?

The fantasy had blown his mind in more ways than one.

Wa-a-ait a minute.

Amanda!

She'd been at the mall. What if she hadn't only just arrived as she had claimed? What if she'd really been shopping, trying on lingerie when he'd walked into the boutique?

She had been the woman he'd been imagining in the fantasy as he'd read it. It had been her his fingertips had been aching to touch.

And that wasn't all that ached, he thought, his hand moving restlessly on his thigh. She had him touching himself, for heaven's sake! He'd need a cold shower to release the sexual tension the letter had aroused.

And then he laughed.

Amanda Butterworth. He wished!

No way was Amanda Butterworth the one sending him the fantasy letters. They rubbed each other the wrong way, he thought with a chuckle.

A damned shame, too.

Standing, he stretched, reaching high into the air above him, his unsnapped khaki shorts slipping low on his lean hips. The moonlight glinted off his body where it wasn't covered in the hair that curled across his chest and arrowed down his hard belly.

He stared sightlessly across the lawn below, not seeing Amanda in the black RX-7 parked there, catching her breath at the sight of his lithe, virile body.

Turning, he picked up the letter and the dishes and went inside. When he'd rinsed the dishes and put them in the dishwasher, he headed for his desk, wrinkling his nose as he slid the center drawer open. His desk was starting to smell very feminine, and he was feeling very masculine.

Remembering the fantasy's suggested remedy, he headed for the bathroom. Yes, a cold shower was exactly what he needed to take care of the way he was feeling, or he'd never get any sleep.

In the bathroom, he unzipped his khaki shorts and let them slide to the cool tile floor. Stepping into the shower, he adjusted the water temperature, then stood beneath the cold, stinging pellets of water to let the remedy do it's work.

Thoughts of red lingerie and black silk stockings slid down the drain with the rivulets of water sluicing off his hard body.

Amanda Butterworth's image wasn't so easily washed away.

She remained on his mind deep into the night as he tossed restlessly in his sleep.

5

NOAH TRENT plopped a peppermint candy into his mouth and looked down at the ratings sheet on his desk. It verified that his decision to make Amanda Butterworth cohost of *Theater Talk* had been a good one. The ratings were up. Kyle and Amanda were clicking with the audience, if not with each other. The upward surge in the ratings had precipitated his calling an impromptu meeting with them.

Rising from his chair with the ratings in hand, he strolled over to the window of his office and looked out over the river he loved. Below he saw Amanda and Kyle approaching as if they were strangers. Their disregard for each other was a little too studied to be convincing.

Moments later Kyle strolled into Noah's office. Resting his hip on the edge of Noah's desk, he took a peppermint candy from the dish by his thigh. He was all effortless charm and teasing sensuality as he watched Amanda enter the office and purposely take a seat across the room from him on the old tweed sofa.

"What's up?" Kyle asked, turning his attention to Noah, who was still standing at the window.

"The ratings are up, that's what," Noah answered, waving the ratings sheet in his hand.

Amanda smiled, openly displaying her pleasure at the news. Rising ratings reflected favorably on her recent addition to the show. She glanced over at Kyle to gauge his reaction to Noah's news..

Kyle caught her glance and sent her a sweet smile that wasn't. Turning back to Noah, he asked, "Does this mean we're getting a raise?"

"You're getting something better," Noah answered. "The two of you are getting a chance at more airtime. Some time has become available on Sunday evening right before the movie. I want you and Amanda to pull together a theme show to put in the empty slot. If you do a good show and it goes over well, I'll consider making it a regular feature."

Noah looked from one to the other. "Either of you have an idea for a theme?"

"How about doing something on foreign films?" Amanda suggested.

Kyle groaned. "We've got to grab the audience's attention, not put them to sleep. I think we should do horror films."

"Yech, you can't be serious about doing a show on those slasher flicks," Amanda objected with disdain, shaking off a shudder.

Kyle moved the candy mint around in his mouth with his tongue as he gave her a long, considering stare. Then he winked. "You can hold on to me if you get scared," he offered, leaving his perch on the edge of Noah's desk to slouch beside her on the sofa, deliberately invading her space.

Noah looked out the window again and closed his eyes on a heavy sigh.

With Noah's attention momentarily diverted, Kyle took advantage of the opportunity to continue annoying Amanda. "I suppose it's too much to hope you're a screamer," he whispered suggestively, giving his evil twin, Lyle, free rein.

Amanda shot up from the sofa, and Kyle's unrepentant chuckle followed her across the room to Noah's desk, where she made a pretense of wanting a mint. Her flushed face gave away the pretense.

"Now, children," Noah said facetiously. Turning from the window, he informed them, "I've just thought of an idea for a theme for the trial show. It's going to be 'Love Scenes,' and the two of you will give the male and female viewpoints on intimacy in the movies."

"I like it," Kyle said, nodding his approval.

They both looked to Amanda.

Amanda shrugged. "As long as he promises not to pick scenes from any of his personal favorites, like *Valley of the Velvet Vixens*."

"*Valley of the*—" Kyle repeated incredulously, his rich, throaty laugh erupting before he finished.

Noah's eyes twinkled with mirth. "What do you say, Kyle?" Noah asked. "Do you agree to Amanda's condition?"

Kyle cleared his throat and looked at Amanda. "I will if you will," he countered, cocky and sure.

"Will what?" Amanda asked, her eyes narrow with suspicion.

"I'll promise to censor my choices if you promise to do horror films next," Kyle answered, pushing his luck.

Amanda shook her head, her eyes rolling ceilingward. "I swear you have the hormones of a sixteen-year-old boy."

"Better than having the hormones of a ninety-year-old spinster," he taunted with a pointed look to the neat bun coiled at the nape of her slender neck.

Noah broke in before there was bloodshed. "You'd both do well to concentrate on this show. If it's not a success, there won't be another to worry about."

"What do you want to do about format, Noah? Stay with the same one we're using now?" Kyle asked.

"No. I thought we'd change things around a bit. I want each of you to pick a couple of favorite scenes as examples of compelling love scenes so the viewers get a sense of the differences in the way men and women view intimacy."

Amanda looked down at her watch.

"Going somewhere?" Kyle asked from the sofa, where he'd made himself so comfortable it didn't look as if he ever planned to move again. The question had been in the form of a challenge.

Ignoring Kyle as if he were a nosy younger brother, Amanda looked to Noah. "I have something scheduled for one," she explained. "Do I need to cancel?"

"No . . . no, I think we've finished here. Go on ahead and keep your appointment. The two of you can get together later today and iron out the details. It would be a good idea to free up the rest of your schedule for the next few days, though. You and Kyle are going to need to burn some midnight oil to get both shows ready on time."

They both watched Amanda's hurried departure, her perfect posture in her neat navy blue suit speaking of attendance at the best finishing schools.

Seeing Kyle's look of frustration, Noah couldn't resist stirring the pot. "Think she's got a hot date for lunch?" he asked.

"More likely an appointment to get her corset laced tighter," Kyle grumbled.

Noah chuckled as he sat down in his chair. "Going that well, is it?"

Kyle's fingers stretched around her imaginary throat. "She drives me crazy," he said through gritted teeth. "Just once I'd like to see her lose that perfect control of hers and let down her hair. It's gotten to the point that that's all I think about."

They sat in silence for a few minutes while Kyle's thoughts drifted to the fantasy letters locked in his desk drawer, their sexy contents never far from his mind. Amanda always starred in the mental playbacks, though he knew that was perverse. No doubt she'd have him arrested if she could read his mind.

Having her on his mind was one thing, but having her on his show was quite another. His evil twin, Lyle, hadn't been any help, pulling that stunt on their first show of agreeing with every one of her reviews. She'd turned the tables on him and used his ploy against him.

He couldn't let her come out on top again. What he needed was an unfair advantage. . . .

Suddenly he sat straight up and snapped his fingers, indicating he'd just had a brilliant idea.

Noah watched him uneasily.

A sly grin teased Kyle's lips. "What would you think, Noah, about doing the theme show unscripted?" he asked.

"Why would you want to do that?" Noah wondered.

"To give the show an added edge," Kyle answered, not voicing another more devious reason.

He knew Amanda would hate the idea. It was hard to be perfect when you were live. He was bound and determined to ruffle her feathers.

AMANDA WAS STILL FURIOUS. She couldn't believe what Kyle had done. At first when he'd told her, she'd thought he was joking.

But he hadn't been.

How dare he go behind her back and get Noah's approval to do the "Love Scenes" theme show unscripted. She was going to look like a fool, she just knew it. She punched the love seat's pillow, pretending it was Kyle. He knew she liked everything planned carefully so there would be no slipups. Knowing that, he'd gone right ahead and proposed his harebrained idea.

It was a low-down, underhanded, yellow-bellied, snake-in-the-grass thing to do. She punched the pillow again and then picked it up and threw it across the room in a temper. There was no way she was going to let Kyle get away with what he'd done unscathed, she vowed.

There was nothing she could do about the show. Noah had already approved Kyle's idea. She'd have to do the show Kyle's way, and he'd no doubt throw her a curve the way he had on their first show. But, she remembered, she'd managed to come out on that show okay, hadn't she?

Feeling better for having recalled how she'd managed to ad-lib her way out of adversity, she got up and paced the floor, chewing her bottom lip.

Kyle's comments about her objection to doing the show unscripted still stung. He'd called her rigid and uptight.

He didn't understand. She was a warm, seductive woman. A woman who sometimes gave in to temptation. Walking over to her desk, she pulled open the drawer where she kept the pale pink stationery and the small bottle of Pleasure perfume. She was going to get even, if only secretly.

AMANDA WASN'T HOME five minutes when the doorbell began it's insistent appeal. She was in no mood to face a salesman. Traffic on the way back from delivering the fantasy letter to Kyle's apartment had been a snarled mess. She had used the knowledge that Kyle was playing in a charity basketball game sponsored by the station to assure she wouldn't be discovered. Glancing down at her silver watch, she saw that the game wouldn't be over for a few minutes.

The cup of tea in her hand clattered to the counter when the salesman began leaning on the doorbell again. After quickly wiping up the spilled tea, Amanda hurried to the door to dispatch him. Kyle wouldn't think she was so ladylike if he could hear the words she was muttering beneath her breath, she thought.

Jerking open the door when she reached it, she made ready to freeze the hapless salesman with a single look.

It was she who froze, instead.

Kyle Fox filled her doorway with a rock star's blatant virility. He was freshly showered, and like the first time she'd seen him, his clean, masculine scent assaulted her senses. She stepped back unconsciously, resisting the urge to touch his still-damp hair curling slightly at the ends.

Why wasn't he at the basketball game? Where had he been when she'd delivered her fantasy letter to his place—in the shower? Had he gotten out to discover who she was and followed her home . . . ?

"Aren't you going to invite me in?" he asked, interrupting her wildly racing imagination.

"Uh . . . yes, of course," she answered, swallowing dryly. A moment later an alarm signal went off in her mind. Oh no. Had she put away the pale pink stationery and the perfume?

She backed toward the desk as he entered.

"How come you didn't come and watch me play in the charity basketball game this afternoon?" he asked.

"Uh . . ." she stammered, feeling behind her to make sure the desk was clear of evidence. "Uh . . . the basketball game?"

"Yeah the charity game KCNX sponsored." He eyed her curiously. "Look, is there something wrong?"

She breathed a sigh of relief when her hands told her the desk was clear. "No. No, of course not. I was napping when you rang the bell is all," she lied, moving away from the desk. "Did you win the . . . ah . . . basketball game?" she asked, taking a seat on the arm of the love seat.

"I don't know. I fouled out and left early after signing autographs for the crowd." His blue eyes twinkled.

"It's not too late for you to get one. I'll even personalize it for you," he offered with a wicked grin as he moved to her desk to get a pen and paper from the drawer.

"No!" Amanda objected, her heart lodging in her throat.

The alarm in her voice stopped him instantly.

He turned and looked at her curiously. "Are you *sure* there's nothing wrong?"

He wasn't a dummy. She had to come up with a better reason for her odd behavior than being sleepy. Flailing around in her mind, she plucked the first reason she came up with that she thought he might buy. "Yes, there is something wrong, and you know good and well what. You purposely went behind my back to get Noah's approval to do the theme show unscripted, and now you come over acting like nothing's changed, offering me your . . . your autograph!"

"Is that all?" he asked, coming to her and lifting her chin with his finger.

"What are you doing?" she demanded, her nerves at the breaking point.

"I'm trying to apologize. Look, I still think my idea is a good one, but you're right. I should have discussed it with you first. That's why I came over, as a matter of fact. I want to take you to dinner as my apology."

"Dinner . . . ?"

"You could try to work up a little more enthusiasm. If I were the sort to get my feelings hurt, I'd be crushed."

"I'm sorry. I wasn't expecting you to apologize."

He mussed her hair. "Yeah, well I'm not the total beast you make me out to be, you know."

Amanda began to get the sinking feeling Kyle was even more dangerous when he was nice.

"Come on, let's go," he said, giving her a little nudge.

She looked down at her clothes.

Kyle caught her look. "You're fine as you are. We're going someplace nice and comfortable. The kind of place you can lean back and kick off your shoes."

"Sounds wonderful. I'm starved," she said, realizing she'd forgotten to eat. Her stomach was having none of her pretense at serenity, so it was just as well. She could relax now and eat; the trickiest part of the evening was behind her.

When they were on their way, she closed her eyes and relaxed, trying to collect herself after Kyle's near-disastrous appearance. The next thing she felt was Kyle shaking her arm gently to wake her. "We're almost there," he said, turning off the radio, which had been his company while she'd dozed.

He made a right turn, and she recognized the street. His street. He pulled into a parking spot in front of his place.

"Why are we stopping at . . ," Amanda prevented herself from saying "your place" just in time. "This place?" she finished. He might become suspicious of her knowing where he lived. With good reason.

"This is Chez Fox," Kyle said with a wink.

"Chez Fox? Is this where you bring all your babes?" she asked, looking sullen.

" 'Babes'?" he mocked, smiling briefly. "No, I never bring a woman here, not one I'm planning to seduce, anyway."

"Why not?"

"Because I like the freedom of being able to leave when I choose," he answered with a shrug.

Suspicion crept into her voice. "Why did you bring me here?"

"Why do you think?" he murmured, leaning close.

Her eyes widened, and he laughed. "Are you always so suspicious? I brought you here to cook for you, what else?"

"*You* can cook?"

"I manage...."

"Pasta?" she asked hopefully.

"You're in luck. That's my speciality."

She was hungry and it would be nice to just relax informally instead of coping with the fuss a restaurant dinner entailed.

Kyle escorted her to the front door. The minute he unlocked it and ushered her inside, she smelled the perfume and remembered what had been niggling at the edge of her mind since she'd awoken from her nap to find them pulling up to Kyle's place.

Before them on the quarry floor lay the scented pale pink envelope. She couldn't have been more alarmed if it had been a coiled cobra.

Her mind raced to think of a way to hide the envelope from Kyle. Her eyes searched for a place to surreptitiously kick it into hiding; there was not a piece of furniture or anything obligingly nearby.

It was too late, anyway. From the corner of her eyes, she saw Kyle reach to retrieve the envelope from the floor.

Her devilish streak asserted itself, since conceal-
ment was lost. Before he could reach it, she snatched
the envelope up.

"What's this?" she asked with feigned innocence.

"A fan letter, I suppose," Kyle answered, taking it
from her and laying it on the coffee table dismissively.

Amanda had a sudden inspiration. "You know, I
think I feel like cooking. It relaxes me sometimes. Why
don't you sit down on the sofa and read your fan letter
while I putter in your kitchen?" she suggested. Her
playful push caught him off guard enough to land him
on the sofa.

Picking up the envelope from the coffee table, she
sniffed it mockingly. "Here, read."

With that she went off to the kitchen humming,
leaving him with the pink envelope in his lap, where
she'd so cavalierly tossed it.

Kyle knew she would think it was strange if he didn't
open the letter. At the very least she'd tease him about
it unmercifully. So with a great deal of trepidation, he
slit the flimsy pink envelope with his forefinger. Pulling out the sheets of stationery, he unfolded them and
swallowed dryly.

Kyle,

I liked the old set of Theater Talk *better. You were so in
control sitting in that wing chair in the mock library.
That's one thing we have in common, Kyle. We both
like Victorian libraries. There's something incredibly
sexy about them, isn't there?*

Maybe it's the red velvet draperies blocking out the real world . . . the smell of leather book bindings . . . the darkened shadows . . . the special books hidden under lock and key. . . .

Let's pretend again, shall we, Kyle? It's winter. You live in a very old country manor house next door to our family. In fact, you're my father's counselor. You do a lot of legal work for my father, and you've begun to notice me.

You know who I am, don't you, Kyle? I'm your neighbor's spoiled daughter. So very spoiled, and I've been teasing you, haven't I? Unmercifully. But you're ten years older than I am. And you would never betray my father's trust, would you?

But you want to, don't you Kyle? You've wanted to for some time now.

There's someone at the door. You'll have to answer it yourself. The help is off for the holidays, and you're all alone in the big old manor house. Hurry and answer the door.

Are you happy to see me, Kyle? I'm home from school for the holidays. My father sent me to deliver some papers he wants you to look over before he adds his signature. Why don't you ask me in to warm myself by the fire in your library? It's very cold outside. The snow is swirling around capriciously behind me as the wind howls its fierce, chilly moan.

Thank you for inviting me in, Kyle. The fire feels so warm against my bare, windburned knees. Aren't you going to offer me a sherry? I need a little courage for what I'm about to do. . . .

Thank you.

You don't mind if I take my coat off, do you? See, I'm still in the uniform of the private girls' college I attend. As a freshman, I have to wear it all the time.

It's very frustrating going to an all-girl school. I can't wait to change out of my school uniform. My white knee socks are constantly slipping down. Oh, you noticed?

Do you mind if I look around your library? This room is so masculine, Kyle. So very like you. And look, you even have a ladder sliding along one wall so you can reach the books hiding on the top shelves. What kind of books do you keep up there, Kyle? Mind if I climb the ladder to see . . . ?

Darn, my knee sock has started to slip again. I don't want to let go of the ladder. Would you mind terribly pulling it up for me, Kyle?.

Kyle? What are you waiting for, an engraved invitation?'

There, that's better. Thank you..

Maybe it's better if I come down the ladder. Kyle, what's the matter? You don't look too steady. Here, let me loosen your tie. You look so uncomfortable. . . . Why, Kyle, you're breathing hard. Are you sure you're okay?

Well, if you're sure. . . . I did come inside to warm my-self by your fire, didn't I? Why don't you put another log on the fire and let's get a big blaze going. There, that's better. I love the way hickory wood smells and crackles in a roaring fire, don't you?

I know all about you, Kyle. I know all your secrets. You've sworn to yourself that you're not going to touch me, haven't you, Kyle?

But what if I want you to touch me?

Do you remember that child's game, "Do you trust me?" Well, I'm going to trust you. I'm going to let you do anything you want to me . . . with your hands, Kyle. But only with your hands. You can't kiss me or any-thing else. You know you want to. You know I'm not a kid. I'm nineteen and I've been away to school.

Umm . . . this fire feels so good and warm, Kyle. Why don't you come closer to the flames and feel the heat. I'm going to face the fire and place my hands up here on the mantel and keep them here. I'm going to stare into the fire and wish you were behind me.

Oh! You are.

I'm a woman, aren't I, Kyle? That's right . . . you have free access to my body with your hands. I won't stop you. My hands will stay up on this mantel as though they were handcuffed there. My wool school sweater is itchy against my bare skin. Bare skin, Kyle.

That's right. There's nothing beneath the wool sweater you are rubbing against my breasts but tender skin aching to be touched. Aching, Kyle.

Feel how your caress of my sweater against my breasts has teased my nipples to hard pebbles. Don't you want to slip your hands under my sweater and glide your long, sensitive fingers to the waiting pucker...?

Yes.... That feels...sooo good. Caress me with your gentle touch. I can feel the smooth nail on your thumb rake playfully across the peak, and I want you to twist it between your fingertips. A little harder. Yes, like that...exactly like that. Oh...Kyle, I've always known you could pleasure me.

I want to feel your mouth's wet caress where your hands are. But no, I won't give in to that desire. Put that thought from your mind or banish it to the edges, where it will hover as you cup and caress me and breathe sweetly against my neck.

No, I won't turn around and look at you. I can't. But, please don't stop. Let your hands wander where they desire. The skirt of my school uniform is rather short, the full pleats granting you easy access to my thighs. All that field hockey we are forced to play at school has made them very firm, don't you agree?

Where are your hands sliding now, Kyle? Are you surprised that my cotton panties are bikini? It makes things easier, doesn't it? I love feeling the slight pressure of the elastic against my belly. I can't move my hands, remember. Why don't you just pull my panties down....

No, don't take them off. I don't want to undress. Just leave them tangled at my knees.

Now, cup the heel of your hand against my pelvis. Come closer, Kyle, and dip my back toward you.... Touch me....

Please... like that. Yes....

I really must go, Kyle. Daddy will be wondering what's kept me.

We'll play again, Kyle....

Kyle put the letter down guiltily, expecting to find Amanda standing over him in disapproval, but she wasn't. She was still in the kitchen; he could hear her banging pots around, and the sweet, spicy aroma of tomato sauce wafted in and made his mouth water.

Suddenly he had an appetite. Not that his other appetites weren't already achingly aroused. He sat there a moment, willing evidence of what he was sure Amanda would view as his depravity to go away. He had an overwhelming desire to kiss her. Amanda had been the girl in the fantasy as he'd read, but there had been no clue to give away the writer as he had hoped. So much for his suspicions.

When he could walk, he got up and locked the letter in his desk drawer with the other two. It wouldn't do for Amanda to pick it up and read it. Much as he would like to think Amanda had been the writer, he was sure she'd be shocked at the blatant sexuality in the writing.

With the letter safely tucked away, he went off to the kitchen, following his nose to the bubbling, spicy sauce cooking on the stove.

He pulled up short when he saw Amanda. She was a sight. Her face was flushed from the steaming water she was preparing the pasta in. Tendrils of her brown hair were coming down from her topknot to lie in wispy layers around the slim column of her neck.

Kyle wanted to lift those tendrils and create a pathway for his lips on her skin, so soft . . . inviting. He slipped into a sexual trance.

Amanda had been wondering what effect her fantasy letter was having on Kyle. This was her first chance to see his immediate reaction up close. It hadn't occurred to her until she'd picked up the envelope that she'd wanted to.

She felt him watching her and looked up. His glazed eyes and sheepish smile told her all she needed to know. He'd liked the fantasy—he'd liked it a hell of a lot. The way he was standing wasn't concealing his arousal very effectively. She tried not to take the scenic route. She wasn't very successful.

The room grew smaller . . . airless . . . as they stood watching each other.

"Do me a favor, Amanda."

Kyle's voice was needy, rich with passion. It flowed over her as she waited for him to ask of her the favor she would be powerless to deny him in that moment.

"Put down that French bread you're buttering . . . and come here."

She didn't move.

"*I said*, come here . . ." Kyle's voice was husky, demanding.

"Just a minute. I've got garlic butter all over my hands," she said, impatiently looking around for something to wipe them on.

Kyle was beside her in two strides. "To hell with the garlic butter. I want—need—to hold you . . . *now*."

Amanda held her greasy, fragrant fingers wide of him as he took her face in his hands and nibbled once before attacking her mouth again and again with eating kisses.

He came up for air, then grabbed her hand, sliding his flattened tongue up her palm and plunging her buttery fingers into his warm, moist mouth.

Amanda shivered.

"This . . . this is what I wanted, Amanda, at the movie theater when our hands kept sliding against each other in the hot, buttery popcorn braced between my thighs."

Amanda's eyes grew wide and bright.

His lips moved to her neck, licking the edges of her silk blouse, edging closer to the subtle cleavage.

"No, don't. I'm ticklish," she pleaded, trying to slap his hands away from the tie there, until she remembered the garlic butter still coating her fingers.

He moved back to her mouth and buried his tongue deep inside, eliciting a breathy moan of desire from her. She didn't give a damn suddenly that she was smearing him with garlic butter as she wrapped her arms around his neck. He backed her up against the refrigerator. Tremors of desire raced along every circuit of her body, tripping every alarm, ringing for an uncaring guard.

"Oh Amanda!" Kyle whispered hoarsely, burying his face against her neck. He ground his hips into hers. "I'm so hot for you."

Amanda froze. Reality intruded with Kyle's words. He wasn't hot for her. He was hot for whoever had written him the fantasy letter. She had written it, of course, but he didn't know that. It could have been anybody. She was just handy, a convenience. He didn't have the same deep feelings for her that she was just now realizing she had unfortunately developed for him.

She twisted from his embrace and raced for the living room.

The pot of pasta on the stove started boiling over, hissing and sputtering like a disapproving chaperon.

Kyle stopped just long enough to turn off the gas beneath the pot.

Amanda scooped up his keys from the coffee table in front of the sofa, where Kyle had dropped them. Her hand was on the front doorknob when he reached the living room.

"I'll drive you home," he said quietly, crossing the distance between them.

"No. Please. I'll see you get your car back in the morning."

Kyle looked into her teary eyes. "Amanda, what just happened . . . I didn't mean . . . I'm sorry." He wiped a tear from beneath her eye with a swipe of his unsteady hand.

He *was* even more dangerous when he was nice.

While she still had the will, she turned and fled.

6

KYLE SPENT THE REST of the evening trying to forget how very good Amanda had felt in his arms. Needs he had long repressed surfaced, bringing painful memories and feelings he'd wanted to keep buried like the treasure of some long lost pirate ship.

Countless times he reached for the phone to call her, but not once did he allow himself to follow the urge. He knew better than to let his heart rule his head.

Amanda had gotten past his better judgment, was all. Perhaps because he had tired some time ago of casual affairs. Not just because they were no longer prudent, but because he'd also come to realize he couldn't live his whole life in pleasant anesthetization.

What was he going to do about her? He had felt the attraction humming between them from the beginning, but he'd denied it to himself, still remaining closed to his feelings. Her responses to his caresses had been those of a hungry woman. But was that all it was— hunger? Would any man have done? At one time that wouldn't have mattered to him, but not any longer. He wanted Amanda to want him and only him.

He had to stop tormenting himself with her.

By the amount of wine left in the bottle, he judged it was a few hours after midnight. He went to his desk and unlocked the drawer where he kept the fragrant fantasy letters. He was unshaved, morose and frustrated as he carried the letters to the sofa, where he lay down to read them. When he finally drifted off to sleep, the third fantasy letter slipped from his fingers to flutter to the floor.

His dreams mirrored the fantasies, but they were all of the woman he was trying desperately to dismiss.

AMANDA SPENT THE NIGHT trying to sort out her emotions. She was in love with Kyle. She wanted him in ways she hadn't imagined. With Kyle it could be the stuff of fantasy. But she was very much afraid it couldn't be the real thing.

He hadn't shown any sign of being the kind of man who made the forever kind of commitment. The kind of man she knew she ultimately needed for true happiness.

"WHERE *IS* HE?" Noah demanded as he came striding into the studio where Amanda and Toby were waiting to tape the theme show.

Looking to Toby, he asked, "Did you hear from him?"

Toby shook his head and looked down to study the schedule in his hand.

"Amanda?"

"No, Noah. I haven't heard from Kyle since we finished blocking out the show last night on the telephone." She hadn't seen him since he'd kissed her senseless. It was her opinion that Kyle was being late deliberately to rattle her. He knew she was nervous about doing the show unscripted. It would be just like him to stroll in one second before they were scheduled to begin taping.

Noah popped an antacid tablet into his mouth. He began chewing, his eyes on the clock. His threat when it came was the idle one of a fond parent. "So help me, if he doesn't show up on time, I'm going to have you do the show with Toby here."

Toby dropped the papers he was shuffling.

At that auspicious moment, Kyle came rushing in looking as though he'd been hit by a truck. There was no blood, but his usually immaculate appearance was replaced by the look of an unmade bed.

"Good Lord, boy, what happened to you?" Noah asked, then before giving Kyle a chance to reply, bellowed, "Makeup!"

Kyle had just finished tucking in his shirttail when the hair and makeup artist appeared with a portable tray. She began flitting around Kyle, getting him ready for the air, while he began an excited, animated recital of his reason for being late and looking a wreck.

"Man, Noah, I thought for a minute there I was going to have to deliver a baby all by myself," he said, his color still on the chalky side.

"A baby," everyone chorused, forgetting they were angry with him.

"Yeah. I started into the station a little early since I knew Amanda was a bit nervous about doing the show unscripted. I had just gotten onto the highway when I saw this lady pulled onto the shoulder. I could see she had a flat tire, so I got out to change it for her. I didn't think anything of it when she didn't get out of the car— just figured she was leery of strange men. When I got the tire changed, I went to tell her she could drive, and that's when I found out she was in labor," he explained.

Amanda noted that Kyle's color was returning as he told of the events, even as Toby was growing paler.

Noah chuckled. "So what'd you do—faint to get out of delivering the baby?"

"Nope," Kyle answered, shaking his head. "I got real lucky. A state patrolman stopped and took over. First time in my life I was ever happy to see the law."

He flashed Amanda a grin and mopped his brow comically.

Amanda couldn't help laughing. She bet he was perfectly precious trying to help the pregnant lady. It was a sight she would have dearly loved to have witnessed. She shook off a pang of guilt for suspecting Kyle of deliberately being late to sabotage her performance. Still, she couldn't help being pleased that now she wasn't the only one who was a little bit flustered.

"Speaking of birthing babies," Noah said, looking down at his watch, "let's see if we can't get this theme show in the can. My stomach will rest a lot easier when I see that this unscripted idea of Kyle's actually works."

The makeup artist finished up with Kyle and dabbed a quick sponge to Amanda's nose and forehead before leaving.

Toby and Noah consulted the schedule while Kyle and Amanda took their places in front of the camera. When they were ready, Toby rechecked to make sure the film clips were in order.

Noah signaled that they were on.

"Tonight's special theme show is called 'Love Scenes,'" Kyle began. "My cohost, Amanda Butterworth, and I are going to explore intimacy—" he paused and gave Amanda a racy look "—in the movies."

"That's right, Kyle." Amanda said, swallowing dryly. "It should be interesting to see the differences and parallels in male and female opinion on what constitutes intimacy." Kyle's racy look had brought his racy kiss swimming to the surface of her mind, and she'd only just managed to get her line out.

Amanda's film clip was the first one up. When it was finished, she turned to the camera. "That, of course, was the first illicit kiss between Zhivago and Lara in *Doctor Zhivago*, a movie famous for showing the obsessiveness of falling in love. How it feels when you can't eat, sleep or think of anyone but the love object. In the movie, Zhivago is compelled beyond reason by his love for Lara," Amanda began.

"You've got to be kidding. You picked a musical?" Kyle interrupted.

Amanda turned to Kyle with a pained expression. With obvious patience, she explained, "*Doctor Zhivago* was *not* a musical."

"Of course it was," he argued. "Every time Zhivago looked at Lara he'd hear that sappy *da-da-da-da*." Kyle's innocent smile was anything but. It telegraphed that he had no intention of behaving himself.

She decided to challenge him rather than further defend her clip. "Okay, then let's see what car chase you found so intimate."

"Now, now . . . don't get tetchy. I picked one I know you'll love. Y'all prepare to swoon now, y'hear?" he teased broadly.

Rhett Butler appeared on the screen in all his roguish charm, sweeping Scarlett up the grand staircase to the bedroom.

The lights came up again. "Didn't I tell you? Isn't that every female's dream—to be swept off her feet by a handsome hero?" Kyle said smugly.

Amanda's pained expression returned. No way was she going to give him his due. "In case you haven't noticed in between watching macho beer commercials," she said with saccharine sweetness, "two things have gone out of fashion since the Civil War—slavery and male dominance."

"What!"

"You heard me. That scene you find so all-fired romantic has nothing to do with intimacy. What it has to do with is a man using superior physical strength against a woman."

"Give me a break." Kyle sighed.

"No. What I'll give you is a true example of intimacy between a man and a woman," Amanda said, nodding to Toby to put up her next film clip.

It was the chess scene from *The Thomas Crown Affair*. They were both lulled into the atmosphere of the film clip, vicariously experiencing the sexual chemistry crackling on-screen between McQueen and Dunaway. Kyle cleared his throat when the film clip was over and muttered, "Talk about not playing fair."

Amanda ignored his comment. "If you noticed, Kyle, no one was coerced in that scene. When the kiss came,

it was something they both wanted with equal desper-
ation."

"Agreed, but the woman in that scene was an honest
woman willing to acknowledge she wanted the man,
willing to take the risk of being openly seductive, unlike Scarlett O'Hara."

"Scarlett lived in a different time," Amanda said by
way of defending her.

"And so did Rhett," Kyle retorted, scoring his point,
as well. He nodded to Toby to bring up his next film
clip.

The beach scene in the movie *From Here to Eternity*
flashed on the screen. Amanda and Kyle each had a little trouble sitting still as they watched the two lovers
on-screen roll in a passionate clinch half-clothed, half
in and half out of the water on the sandy beach.

When the lights came back up, Amanda looked over
at Kyle nervously.

His shrug was elegant as he faced the camera un-
abashed. "A little sand, a little water, a whole lot of
heat . . . What can I say?"

Amanda didn't . . . couldn't say anything. Her breath
was still caught in her throat.

"Your turn," Kyle said, leaning back in his seat and
daring her to top his clip.

Amanda nodded to Toby to bring up her next clip.
It was really not one but two clips from the same movie.
First up was the grand sweep of the coastline and an old
priest warning the young woman married to the older
man to be careful what she wished for. It was immediately followed by another clip showing what she
wished for getting off the stagecoach as the camera

panned lovingly up the tall black boots of the young, virile army officer.

"Sometimes," Amanda said when the lights came up, "intimacy and the temptation of the forbidden are one and the same."

"I'm amazed!" Kyle burst out in surprise.

"Amazed . . . ?" Amanda asked hesitantly, wary of where Kyle was leading her, as it was usually down the garden path.

This time he was being serious, though. *"Ryan's Daughter?* A movie with one of the most visually beautiful love scenes ever filmed, and you didn't pick that clip to show. Why?" he asked with real curiosity, intrigue even.

Amanda's answer was quiet but filled with conviction. "Yes, I agree the love scene in *Ryan's Daughter* was beautiful. But the real intimacy in this movie is in the clips I chose. They dealt with a woman making a choice based on desire. Of course, because of the time period, she was punished. But now, in modern times, we are dealing with women able to financially take care of themselves. Women are now choosing partners for the same reasons men always have . . . desire and physical beauty. And we're making some of the same mistakes."

"What's wrong with choosing a partner based on desire and beauty?" Kyle objected.

"Nothing. As long as it's not the only basis. There has to be more for true intimacy, don't you agree?"

She could see he hadn't been ready for her question.

"Uh . . . well, yes . . . of course."

"I believe it's your turn," she said, tucking a loose tendril behind her ear as he stared at her.

"My turn. Uh, yeah, right." He nodded to Toby.

A New Orleans accent whispered from the screen as one of the hottest young movie actors worked magic beneath the hiked skirt of an equally sexy young actress.

Amanda moaned inwardly, squirming in her chair.

She looked up to catch Kyle watching her. He mouthed the words "Hot stuff, huh?" and winked. He couldn't have caught her more off guard if he'd slid his own hand under her skirt.

The movie he'd chosen was her favorite of the more recent movie releases. Every time the sexy actor used a Cajun endearment, she melted. The movie oozed sexuality, and the chemistry between the costars burned up the screen. Kyle was right. That love scene was *hot stuff*, indeed.

She glanced back at him. He was still watching her, the thoughts behind his blue eyes scorching the air between them. Him and his unscripted, unprincipled ideas!

Murder, she thought. Yes, murder would be nice. She was going to kill him right after the taping was over.

" . . . now can you, Amanda?"

The clip had ended and he'd been asking her a question.

"What?" she asked, at a loss to recall what he'd said.

"I was asking," Kyle said, his eyes twinkling, "if you could complain about the love scene. The man was gentle and only coaxed the woman into letting herself go with her feelings. You don't call gentle coaxing 'male dominance,' I hope?"

"No. No. The love scene was...fine." *Somebody turn off the lights and let's all go home. No, everybody else go home. Everybody except Kyle.* She wanted him to stay. She was still going to kill him, but maybe she'd wait till *after*, like a black widow spider. First she'd play with him awhile. Enjoy herself. After all, he did kiss so very nicely. Well, not nicely, exactly—

"Amanda. You're...ah...next," Kyle said, interrupting her daydream, his grin altogether too smug and satisfied.

Amanda remembered what her last clip was, and her smile matched Kyle's for smugness. She had promised Kyle she wouldn't use an obvious male sex symbol if he wouldn't. She'd lied. Her last clip came on-screen showing one in all his golden glory augmented needlessly by cowboy regalia.

"Hey! No fair—you promised," Kyle whispered from off camera indignantly.

Amanda showed him she was no stranger to elegant shrugs herself.

It was her opinion one could tell a lot about a woman by the scene she preferred in *Butch Cassidy and the Sundance Kid*. There were women, she knew, who preferred the bicycle scene with Butch Cassidy. For her there was no contest. A woman would have to be dead not to melt at the visual thought of Sundance holding a gun on her and ordering her to strip.

The lights came up, and she still had a silly, dreamy smile on her face.

"Now wait a minute!" Kyle objected. "You don't call *that* male dominance!"

"Uh-uh."

"He's holding a gun on her!"

"Uh-huh."

"What?" Kyle demanded in frustration. "He's got some special exemption or something?" His hands were measuring her throat again...and then her waist...and... He shifted uncomfortably in his seat. The sexy scene between the outlaw and the school-marm hadn't been without it's effect on him. More than anything he wished he had a gun and Amanda alone so he could persuade her into letting down her hair as Sundance had done with the schoolmarm.

A light dawned as he thought about it. "Oh, I get it. It's because they're sharing and acting out a fantasy, right?"

Amanda nodded.

"So, you like *fantasies*, do you?" Kyle taunted, making her blanch. "In that case, you'll love my final clip," he said, nodding to Toby to bring it up.

The lights went low. Kyle's final example was a se-ries of clips from one movie. They showed a thief breaking into a woman's apartment and accidentally stealing her journals of private thoughts with the loot. The thief then became obsessed with making her fan-tasies come true and began using them to seduce her.

Because the film was relatively contemporary, there were flashes of nudity, soapy water slipping over bare skin, hands gripping metal headboards and deep, eat-ing kisses.

Toby almost forgot to stop the projector.

Noah wasn't exactly sure it would get past the cen-sors, but he was certainly going to give it a try.

Kyle hadn't done himself any favors. Thank heaven he'd worn pleated pants. He was in pain.

Amanda could only think of the fantasies she'd written Kyle to taunt him and wonder if he was baiting her now. Had he guessed that she was the one behind the letters? She was thankful it was the final clip and she could escape soon. With all her might, she willed Kyle to wrap the show without any comments about the film clips from the movie.

She must have forgotten to click her heels, she thought sardonically when her wish wasn't granted.

"I think this movie about sums it up as the ideal for both sexes," Kyle began. "I'm sure my cohost will agree that women wish men could read their minds." His voice was pure velvet over fine sandpaper as he added, "And men wish they could read women's minds, as well, especially ones with thoughts as seductive as the heroine's private journals reveal in this movie."

Amanda couldn't leave well enough alone. "You've got to be kidding!"

"Now what?"

"How can you condone the hero using the heroine's own private journals to seduce her, as though they were some sort of . . . of . . . *engraved invitation*?"

The unusual phrase might have escaped Kyle's notice. But the sudden look of guilt on Amanda's face triggered his recall of the same phrase in the most recent fantasy from his phantom correspondent.

A hotshot grin leaped to his lips. "'Engraved invitation'?" he repeated, pouncing on her slip of the tongue.

"I meant—"

"You meant it would have been an invitation to seduction only if she had purposely given him the fantasies to read?" Kyle challenged.

"Ah . . ." Amanda stalled, floundering.

"I've got you anyway, my pretty," Kyle said with villainous relish, enjoying watching her squirm. Now he was certain she was the one sending the fantasies. Turning to the camera, he explained, "The hero falls in love with the heroine, and as well we all know, all's fair in love and war."

"That's a wrap," Noah called, cutting off the taping.

Amanda avoided Kyle's eyes as Noah joined them.

"Your unscripted idea shows promise. If this goes over well, we'll try the next one unscripted, also," Noah said.

While Noah had Kyle buttonholed, Amanda inched her way over to the door, planning on slipping out before Kyle noticed she was gone.

She reached the door safely only to be brought up short.

"I want to talk to you," Kyle said, his grip firm on her elbow.

It was apparent talk wasn't all he wanted to do as he steered her into a deserted hallway and backed her up against the wall. He anchored her in place by planting his hands on either side of her head.

"I thought you wanted to—"

He cut off her words, lowering his lips to hers as he had that first day outside Noah's office.

Only this time he brought his body with him, flat up and hard against hers. Slowly and with great expertise, he began kissing her senseless. The kiss exposed all sorts of truths they'd been hiding from each other, and yet it was a kiss neither of them could quite bear to end.

When he pulled back, his eyes were steely blue and hot.

"You *owe* me," he whispered hoarsely.

"Owe you!" The remark snapped her out of the sensual fog he'd wrapped her in. "I don't *owe* you anything," she vowed through her anger and embarrassment.

"Oh yes you do," he differed, running a trembling forefinger down her jaw. "You owe me, all right. You owe me for all the nights you and your provocative fantasy letters kept me tossing and turning and . . . frustrated."

"You frustrate me just as much," she threw back, meaning working with him and his attitude.

He turned her accusation to his advantage. "Does that mean you fantasize about me, too?" he asked, twisting his hips for emphasis while his eyes did wicked things to her jangling nerve endings.

"No!" she answered a little too quickly for it to be the truth.

She saw he wasn't buying the lie she was trying so hard to sell. "I meant . . ." she began, trying to explain about working with him.

But Kyle lowered his head again and hushed her explanation with the barest brush of his lips on hers. "There's nothing wrong with fantasies," he whispered, his lips trailing to the tender spot on her neck just under her ear. His breath was warm and his tongue moist as he nibbled at her ear. "They are even more exciting—" his tongue flicked inside her ear and she moaned "—if you share them . . . act them out."

Desire curled through her as his whispered words crawled inside her mind, temptation incarnate. She wanted to cross her legs to still the aching sensation building there. Surely any moment she would slide right down the wall into a puddle at his feet.

Like a drowning woman, she fought for air and tried to escape a certain fate. "Look, I'm sorry I sent you the fantasy letters—"

"I'm not," he said, cutting off her apology. "As a matter of fact," he said, shooting her a crooked grin and a sexy wink, "I've got a hot-pink swimming suit cut to there with your name on it."

"You've . . ." She swallowed the lump that threatened to cut off the air to her lungs. "But I didn't mean—"

"Oh yes, you did." He was having none of her denial. His hand unfastened the clip that held her hair in place, and slipped it into his jacket pocket. His fingers then slid through her glossy brown tresses. Catching them up in a twist at the back of her head, he held her captive. "You want to do all those sexy things you wrote me in those hot letters, or you wouldn't have thought of them."

Her breathing was shallow and her eyes were wide, mirroring her sexual excitement. Her mouth was soft and swollen from the ravishment of his hungry kiss. The filmy silk of her blouse lifted and fell with her quick breaths.

His eyes narrowed in speculation. "You don't really dislike me at all, do you? All this icy aloofness is just a sham of yours, an act to cover the real you. An act you've been putting on to convince me, but you're not even doing a very good job of convincing yourself, are you?"

His eyes searched her face, lingering on her lips while her gold ankle bracelet twinkled in his memory like an erotic charm. Was she a witch? He was certainly under her spell. He'd never been so lost.

Desire, naked and exposed, flared in his eyes. "I don't know what your game is, but as of right now, I'm playing." With that, he leaned closer, his breath fanning her face. "Admit it," he demanded fervently, "you want me every bit as much as I want you, don't you?"

Amanda wilted under his intense scrutiny, her eyes fluttering closed. His thigh had somehow insinuated itself between hers, and he was pressing his point home very convincingly. She did want him.

"Oh, here you are—" Toby said, coming around the corner and strangling off the last of his sentence when he suddenly realized the intimate scene he'd walked into. Turning bright red, he haltingly managed the message he'd been sent to deliver.

"Uh, sorry. Uh . . . Noah wanted to, uh . . . see you when you're . . . finished. Uh . . . I mean . . . that is . . . before you leave, Kyle."

Noah's message delivered, Toby fled under Kyle's dark, murderous stare.

Time returned to normal from its snail's pace, and the activity of the television station came into focus as they both remembered where they were and how public a place it was.

After a moment, Kyle slowly untangled himself from Amanda and moved back. Taking a deep breath, he raised his eyebrows and reached into his jacket pocket to retrieve her hair clip. He considered it a moment, then returned it to his pocket.

Her eyes questioned his action.

His elegant shrug put in another appearance. The noise of the station faded briefly into the background again as he said, "I like you with your hair all-" he threaded his fingers through it wonderingly "—all free and wild."

His eyes lowered then to a sleepy bedroom half-mast as he considered her while she tried unsuccessfully to return her breathing to normal.

Before he turned to go and find Noah, he left a message of his own. "This isn't over. It hasn't even started yet."

AMANDA PICKED UP the bottle of perfume in her desk drawer and sniffed it's fragrance. She ran her finger over the name on the bottle.... Her plan had backfired. Her secret fantasy letters were a secret to Kyle no longer, and *she* was the one who was obsessed. Had been from the beginning, if she was honest with herself. She hadn't stood a chance against her wildly charismatic cohost. It had been naive of her to believe she had. She was just like all the other fans Kyle was used to swooning at his feet.

Throughout the week he had made several attempts to continue where they'd left off when Toby had interrupted them after the taping of the theme show. She had avoided his advances, because she suspected Kyle didn't take the women in his life seriously. Kyle not taking her seriously was something she knew she wouldn't be able to bear.

Setting the perfume back in the drawer, she walked over to the T.V. and turned on KCNX. *Theater Talk* would be on in a few minutes, and she wanted to watch the theme show they'd taped. If only she hadn't used that phrase, Kyle wouldn't have found out she'd been the one sending him the sexy fantasies. Fantasies he'd taken as an *engraved invitation* to a seduction. A seduction she had to admit she wanted...but she wanted so much more.

The few men in her life back East had taken her seriously, they just hadn't been responsive to her deep sexuality. She wondered if she was being unrealistic to want a man who could fulfill all her needs. Still, in an age when there seemed to be a shortage of available men, she refused to make her only requirement be that the man was breathing.

KYLE SLOUCHED ON HIS SOFA in frustration. He couldn't understand Amanda's reluctance to give in to the simmering attraction between them. Didn't she realize that what they had didn't happen all that often? He threw a sofa pillow across the room. She was without a doubt the most infuriating woman he'd ever known.

He reached for the remote control and turned on KCNX to watch the theme show they had taped earlier in the week.

The beer in his hand never made it to his lips as he became engrossed in watching the byplay between himself and Amanda on the screen. It had been a good show, he judged as he watched the film clips come and go. Amanda had . . . He sat up a little straighter and watched intently as an idea began to take form in his mind.

Yes. . . . Delight lit up his eyes, and his smile grew wider and ever more wicked as he contemplated his idea to penetrate Amanda's defenses. He fully intended to quiet her misgivings about him, to show her he wasn't the ruthless cad she insisted on seeing him as. Of course, what he was about to do was a bit underhanded, but there were times when desperate measures were called for, and this was one of them.

There was no way he was going to let things go on as if nothing had happened between them.

7

NOAH LOOKED UP from studying the station's new budget spread out on his desk as Amanda took a place on the end of the sofa and Kyle strolled over to help himself to a mint.

"What's this you're bloodying up?" Kyle asked, picking up a page of the budget Noah had been working on with a red pen.

"The budget," Noah answered, grabbing the paper away from Kyle's hand.

Kyle plopped the mint he'd unwrapped into his mouth and pushed it to one side. "I hope you're robbing Peter to pay Kyle."

Noah snorted. "I'm robbing everybody to pay Kyle."

Kyle chuckled and looked over at Amanda. "And you're robbing me to pay Amanda. But I don't mind. I'm such a pussycat." When neither of them leaped to negate his outrageous assessment, he pushed his luck. "Why, I think having a cohost is just peachy keen."

Amanda studied her fingernail while Noah studied Kyle.

"Do you have a death wish?" Noah asked finally.

Kyle feigned an innocent schoolboy look, and Noah got down to the business at hand. "As you both know, the theme show got promising reviews and ratings, and we'll no doubt be doing more of them in the future.

Amanda, I've already talked to Kyle about an idea I have to promote *Theater Talk* and build on the popularity the two of you seem to be generating."

A roguish grin creased Kyle's face as he looked to Amanda. "He wants us to start dating. . . . You know, like movie stars do to promote their new movies."

"What!" Amanda stared at Kyle, dumbstruck.

"Ah, see, I told you, Noah. You'd have to give her a raise to get her to agree to date me, and the old budget there doesn't look too promising. You see, she doesn't like me. Hard to imagine, isn't it?" Kyle said with genuine puzzlement.

"Not at this particular moment." Noah sighed. Looking to Amanda, he explained, "That's not my idea at all. Now, Kyle, will you please go sit down and listen?"

"Sure," Kyle agreed with a sloppy salute as he turned and strolled over to where Amanda sat on the sofa. Flashing her a devilish wink, he slouched down only centimeters away from her. Since she was already hugging the arm, she had to endure his nearness or make an obvious move away from him, and she wasn't about to give him the satisfaction of knowing how much he disturbed her.

Watching them, Noah pulled open his desk drawer. He replaced the mint in his mouth with an antacid tablet and began again.

"The Academy Awards will be on next week, and I've got the approval from the powers that be for KCNX to sponsor a contest for the viewers of *Theater Talk*. The station is going to have ballots printed up and distributed to merchants around town. Viewers can then mark the ballots with their picks for the Oscar winners of the major awards. The viewer coming closest to naming all the winners will win a trip to Hollywood."

Toby interrupted, sticking his head in the doorway. "Kyle, the weather guy just came in and said someone's towing your car away."

"Yeah, right," Kyle said, knowing the weatherman's penchant for practical jokes.

Amanda seized the opportunity to get away from Kyle's unnerving nearness. Going over to the window, she looked down. "Did you park your Mustang in front of the fire hydrant, where you always do?" she called over her shoulder.

"Yeah, but it's no sweat. I know the cops on the beat, and they never bother me about it."

"Then you must have forgotten to make your payment. . . ."

"What are you talking about?"

"Well, somebody's hooking your car up to tow, and they're not being real careful—oops! There goes the fender."

"What? Noah, I'll be right back," Kyle promised, sprinting from the room.

Amanda turned from the window and strolled across the room to perch on the edge of Noah's desk, a broad smile on her face as she helped herself to one of his mints.

"That's not very nice, you know, smiling over someone's misfortune," Noah said with mock chastisement, his own smile matching hers.

"I know," she said with a nod. "He's going to be even more ticked when he gets all the way down there," she added, plopping the mint into her mouth, her eyes twinkling with mischief.

"Why? What's going on?"

"Oh nothing," she answered innocently. "Nothing at all."

Noah leaned back in his chair. "His car's not really being towed, is it?" he said, catching on.

"Uh-uh."

"Amanda!"

"What?" she asked, moving the mint around in her cheek with her tongue.

"Nothing." Noah chuckled. "I'm glad to see you're giving him back some of his own."

"It's only fair," Amanda said.

"True, but don't forget, you're the one who's got to work with him when he gets back in a foul mood."

"He's always in a foul mood when he doesn't get his way," Amanda answered, showing a studied lack of concern. "Speaking of work," she said, getting up and walking over to the window again. "I've got an idea about the contest, if you're open to suggestions."

"I'm always open to suggestions, you know that."

"Well, you know that controversy I promised you?"

"Yes."

"I was thinking. . . . What if Kyle and I did a show where we each made our own predictions as to the Oscar winners?" she ventured. "Sort of an adjunct to the contest."

"Pair you off against each other, you mean?"

"That's right. There's enough of an element of unpredictability to the Oscars to make them hard to call, and besides, Kyle and I aren't any more likely to agree about them than we do about anything else."

Noah nodded as he thought about the possibilities. "You know, I like it. It's a fun idea, and it would be a great lead-in show for Oscar night."

After glancing down at his watch to check the time, he looked back up at Amanda.

"Tell you what. I've got a budget meeting in a few minutes. Why don't you go on down and make peace with Kyle by telling him I've agreed to give you a special show on Oscar night."

From her spot by the window, Amanda saw Kyle head back to the building from his car. His determined pace didn't bode well for her. He looked like a man intent on getting even.

"Thanks, Noah, for the vote of confidence," she said, heading out the door.

"No thanks needed," Noah replied, waving her off. "The two of you are doing a good job together."

Amanda stood in the deserted hallway, awaiting the elevator. Toby and the weatherman had disappeared like cowardly lions, leaving her to face Kyle alone. No problem, she reassured herself, armed with Noah's news to defuse him.

When the elevator finally arrived, it's door slid open to reveal one unhappy passenger whose blue eyes lit up when they saw her. Kyle's smile was more a lick of his chops.

It was everything Amanda could do not to back away.

"Going down?" he asked, holding the door, his eyes locking with hers seductively.

She swallowed and nodded.

"Good, I like how you apologize," he said, pulling her into the elevator.

Amanda closed her eyes as the door slid shut behind her. She wasn't claustrophobic, but the look on Kyle's face had told her she had reason to worry about being alone in the small enclosure with him. He had every intention of getting his own back.

Her eyes flew open a few seconds later when the elevator came to an abrupt halt between floors.

"What happened? Are we in trouble?" she asked, her eyes wide with concern.

Kyle leaned against the wall, his hand cocked on his hip as his back shielded the control panel. "You are," he drawled, scattering goose bumps up her arms.

"Me? But it was the weatherman's—"

"Amanda..."

"What?"

"Come here."

"Why?"

"You know why."

"I do?"

"You do."

"Oh."

She took a few hesitant steps toward him, her face flushed. The Muzak was drifting a saxophone solo around them, pulling the tension even tighter.

"Now apologize," he said hoarsely, his forefinger trailing down the side of her neck.

"I'm... I'm sorry," she stammered.

"Uh-uh. Show me," he whispered.

"Show you?"

"Show me."

"How?"

"You know how."

"I do?"

"You do."

"Oh."

Amanda shook her head and came out of the sensual trance Kyle had spun between them. "Look, I'm not kissing you or...or anything. I said I'm sorry and that's my apology."

"Amanda..."

"What?"

"Come here."

"Kyle..."

"*I'm* not pushing any buttons until you push one—" he winked wickedly "—or maybe two of mine."

"Kyle!"

"I'm waiting...." His hand slid behind her neck to coax her forward.

"*One* kiss," she offered, wanting the kiss as much as he did.

"Two," he bartered.

"One," she repeated, standing firm.

"Stingy little thing, aren't you?" he teased.

"One," she said again.

His gaze was direct. "Okay, one... and a half."

"'A half'? What's 'a half'?" she asked as his lips descended.

His hand caressed her breast through her silky blouse by way of explanation, scratching the lace of her bra over her nipple erotically. With a low groan, he pulled her against him.

The floor fell out from under them.

"Damn!" Kyle swore, turning to stop the button he'd activated by backing into the control panel.

He was too late.

The elevator swooshed to a stop at the entrance floor and the door slid open to waiting passengers.

Kyle shot Amanda a wry look. "This is *not* my day."

She suppressed a giggle and scrambled from the elevator, blushing profusely, with Kyle close on her heels.

"Miss Butterworth, wait up!" someone called from behind them as they were about to exit the building.

When she turned, Amanda saw Toby rushing from another elevator. Catching up to them, he explained there was a call for her on line three.

Amanda excused herself and went to take the call at the main floor reception.

"Who was it?" Kyle asked as Toby turned to go.

Toby turned back to Kyle and shrugged, "Some guy."

"Local call?" Kyle asked with studied casualness.

"No, long distance, I think. That's why Noah sent me down to catch her before she left."

Kyle nodded. "Think it's her boyfriend?" he asked with a locker-room leer.

"Miss Butterworth's?" Toby said, his surprised tone of voice expressing his doubt.

"What, Toby? You don't think she had any boyfriends back East?"

"I never really thought about it," Toby answered. "Yeah, I suppose so. She's real pretty and all, it's just..."

"She's a little on the uptight side, right?" Kyle finished for him with a wink of camaraderie.

Their conversation was aborted by Amanda's return.

"Anybody I know?" Kyle asked when she joined him and Toby ran to catch an elevator back up.

"What?" Amanda asked, caught off guard by his question. "Oh . . . ah . . . no," she answered, hoping she wasn't lying.

"Is there anything I should know?" he asked when they were outside the building.

"Anything you should know?" she repeated, a nervous tremor in her voice.

Kyle looked at her curiously. "Yeah, you know, about the meeting with Noah."

"Right, the meeting. Yes, as a matter of fact, there is. Why don't we have lunch together and discuss it?" she suggested, wanting to be in a crowd, where he couldn't make a fuss when she told him about pitching her idea to Noah and getting his approval.

"Let me get this straight. You're asking me to lunch?"

Amanda nodded.

His eyes twinkled. "Must have been some kiss, huh?" he said, referring to their embrace in the elevator.

"Don't flatter yourself. I'm hungry, that's all."

"I noticed," he growled somewhere around the vicinity of her ear, though she felt it's vibration in the pit of her stomach.

"If you don't behave, I won't take you anywhere," she warned.

"But I'm at my best when I'm misbehaving."

"Kyle!"

"Okay, where do you want to eat? My place?"

"Not your place," she objected, remembering the lovemaking that had almost occurred in his kitchen.

"Your place?" he suggested hopefully.

"Not there, either." It was equally as dangerous. The kiss they had shared in the elevator had her hormones zinging through her system. It wasn't fair that one man should have so much sex appeal.

"Where, then?"

"How about the food court at the mall? I've got two movies yet to review for the show, so it would be convenient."

She didn't fool him.

"Chicken," he taunted, knowing she wanted a crowd around.

Amanda narrowed her eyes, wishing he hadn't dared her. From childhood, dares had always been a particular weakness of hers, part and parcel of her stubborn streak.

Kyle took advantage of her hesitation. "I was thinking of something a little sexier. . . ."

"No doubt," she said dryly.

"Woman, you've got the dirtiest mind, I swear. Food. I was talking about food." The corner of his lips lifted. "You see, I have this unsatisfied craving for pasta."

She saw, all right. She knew all about unsatisfied cravings. He hadn't forgotten that night in his kitchen any more than she had, she was secretly pleased to note.

"Okay," she said, giving in to impulse. "Pasta it is. Tell me where there's a good place and give me directions on how to get there, and I'll meet you."

"I've got a much better idea. Why don't you just leave your car here and come with me. I'll bring you back later," he promised, taking her arm possessively and steering her toward his car.

She hated that she liked it.

THE RESTAURANT was in an ethnic neighborhood of long, narrow houses with immaculate postage-stamp yards. Specialty food shops, bakeries and Catholic churches gave the neighborhood a European feel.

When they got inside the restaurant, Amanda's mouth began watering at the aromas of spicy authentic sauces and fresh baked bread that permeated the air.

The owner greeted Kyle with warm hugs and Amanda with extravagant compliments, then showed them to a private booth. The table was laid with white linen instead of the red-and-white checkered tablecloth Amanda had been expecting with her pasta. She knew instinctively this was one of those word-of-mouth gourmet restaurants.

"I fix you something special, Kyle, eh?" the owner said.

Kyle looked to Amanda to see if she was game.

She nodded and the owner hurried off to the kitchen.

"So what do you think?" Kyle asked into the stillness of the room, reaching for her hand across the table.

She pulled her hand back and hid it in her lap. "It's dark," she said, and eyeing the empty tables, added, "and very private."

The owner returned with glasses and a bottle of wine. He pulled up a chair from a nearby table and joined them. Opening the bottle of wine, he poured three glasses and lifted his. "So I think we drink a toast to your beautiful new partner, no?"

"You watch the show?" Amanda asked, lifting her glass to join them.

"But of course. My wife, Rosa, she no miss. She think Kyle here is a, how you say, punk?"

"Hunk." Amanda quickly volunteered the proper word and just as quickly wished she hadn't when she glanced over to see the look of smug amusement on Kyle's face.

Worried that he might have offended Amanda, the owner added, "Oh, but Rosa, she like you, too. Very much. She say you two good together."

"That's what I've been trying to tell her," Kyle muttered.

"What?" the owner asked, not catching Kyle's meaning.

"Amanda here thinks I'm a pain," Kyle explained.

The man chuckled. "Oh, yeah. You are." He looked to Amanda. "But is okay. His heart in right place." With that, the owner drained the rest of the wine in his glass and hurried off to the kitchen to check on the special dish he was preparing for them.

Kyle picked up the thread of their abandoned conversation. "Don't worry, the food here is excellent. The reason the place is deserted is because the restaurant doesn't open until four o'clock. The owner makes an exception in my case."

"You like breaking rules, don't you?" Amanda observed.

"Sure. That's what they're for, aren't they?"

"No. Rules have a reason for being. They are for everyone's protection."

"Is that why you have so many of them? Is it because you're afraid of me? Or is it because you're afraid of yourself?"

Sparks flashed in her eyes. She kept her voice low, but her words were clipped as she expressed her frustration to him. "I don't know why you persist in seeing me as some scared virgin who's afraid of men. I'm not. I like men just fine, and I like sex just fine. So knock it off."

Kyle was silent for a moment, absorbing her tirade. "You're very pretty when you're angry, you know," he said, only half-teasingly.

"That's an old line and you know it," she said, refusing to take the bait.

"Okay, here's a new one," he began, lifting his wineglass to toast her. "To the prettiest cohost I've ever had."

Amanda laughed.

"I'm the *only* cohost you've ever had."

"Picky, picky," he retorted.

He swirled the remaining wine in his glass, then glanced back up at her as he took a drink. Setting the glass down, he waited.

"What?" she asked with a giggle, beginning to feel the giddy effect of the wine.

"It's your turn," he explained.

"My turn?"

"Yes. Aren't you going to say something nice about me now . . . like I'm the handsomest cohost you've ever had?" he teased.

"I've had other cohosts," she lied, feeling mischievous.

"Did you date them?" he asked with studied casualness.

"Who?"

"These guys who were handsomer than me."

"Oh, them. I dated a few handsome guys, sure."

"And . . ."

"And nothing."

"You didn't fall in love with any of them?"

"No." She shrugged. "There was always something missing."

"Yeah. I know what you mean."

"Why are you so interested in my love life?" she asked, the wine making her brave.

"I don't know. Maybe I'm just trying to figure out why you don't like me," he suggested, continuing to absently run his finger around the rim of his wineglass.

"I like you." The "I don't trust you" was understood. "I thought we came here to talk about what Noah and I discussed."

Kyle leaned back in his chair. The subject of her liking him was obviously closed. "Okay, shoot. Tell me what you cooked up with Noah while I was off on that wild-goose chase."

"I didn't cook up anything. And the lie about your car being towed was an impulse. While you were checking it out, I got an idea and suggested it to Noah, is all. I thought it would be fun to do a special show for the Academy Awards with each of us making our own set of predictions as to who would win the major awards on Oscar night."

"You did what!" Kyle demanded, sitting up straight.

"I just told you."

"I know what you said. I just can't believe you went behind my back to Noah with an idea for a show without discussing it with me first."

"Why? It's no different than you getting approval from Noah for doing the theme show unscripted without discussing it with me first, except that I didn't do it on purpose. It just happened."

"I apologized for that," Kyle said, as if it exonerated his act.

"Okay. I apologize. I should have waited for you to return before I talked to Noah. I'm sorry."

"Here we are," the owner said, setting down two plates of pasta and a basket of rolls. Curls of heat steamed up to tantalize them, and their argument was forgotten as they buttered hot, crusty rolls and spun the angel hair pasta around on their forks.

"Umm, this is heaven," Amanda said with a sigh, slipping her fork from her mouth. Kyle swallowed and gave the dish his finger-to-thumb circle of approval.

The owner smiled happily, pleased with their obvious delight in his cooking. "You eat. Rosa, she make special dessert," he said, heading back to the kitchen.

"Dessert?" Amanda said questioningly to Kyle, eyeing the plate of pasta in front of her.

"Yeah. You don't walk out of here, you roll out," he answered, lifting his glass of wine.

They ate in silence, the aroma and taste of the food stimulating their appetites, making them more ravenous than when they came in. The only sounds were the light opera playing over the sound system in the background and the occasional clink of a fork against a plate.

Kyle finished and sat watching Amanda.

When she was two-thirds done, she sat back and wiped her lips with her napkin. "Kyle, I can't possibly finish this and eat dessert, too."

He winked and switched his empty plate with hers. "More wine?" he asked, topping off his.

She held her hand over her glass and shook her head. "I'm already dizzy as it is."

"About your idea for this awards show," Kyle began as he started to finish up the pasta.

"Don't you think it's a good idea?" she asked.

"Yes," he agreed reluctantly. Unable to finish the last few bites, he pushed his plate away. "It's a good idea." He sat back in his chair, sipping his wine and watching her.

She began squirming anxiously. "What?" she asked, finally unable to bear his amused scrutiny any longer.

"I was just thinking. You know I'm going to beat the pants off you, don't you?"

"I don't know any such thing," she objected. "In fact, I rather think it's going to be the other way around. It's me who's going to be leaving you in my dust."

Those were exactly the words he wanted to hear. No fool, he had always known there was something missing from all his relationships with women. But until he'd met Amanda, no woman had ever seemed to want more from him than his good looks and sexy body. He knew that to get Amanda's trust, he had to make her vulnerable to him, make her see there was a sensitive man beneath the public figure he presented.

To do that, he had to get close to her, and her professional confidence had led her right into his well-laid trap. The one he had been planning since viewing the theme show.

Lifting his glass, he stared at her over the rim raising his eyebrow as he considered her. Finally he voiced his challenge as if it had just occurred to him instead of being carefully planned.

"If you're so all-fired confident in your ability to make a better showing than me in choosing the Oscar winners, perhaps you'd like to place a side bet with me to make things interesting."

"You're on," she agreed impulsively. "Let's say a hundred dollars?"

Kyle shook his head.

"More?"

"I thought we agreed to make things interesting," he challenged.

"What, then?"

He studied her through narrowed eyes.

"What?" she demanded.

"Suppose we each write down a fantasy and seal it in an envelope that we bring with us on Oscar night. After we tape the show, we can go back to your place and watch the Academy Awards on TV to see which of us picked the most winners. Then . . ."

"Then . . . ?"

"The loser has to act out the winner's fantasy."

"No way."

Kyle could tell she was intrigued by the idea nonetheless. "I thought so. What happened to that ability you were so all-fired sure of? If you were really confident, you'd agree to the bet because you wouldn't be afraid of losing."

"Okay. It's a bet! Are you satisfied?" she fumed, taking his dare, unable to bear his smug gloating a second longer.

Satisfied? No. Not yet, Kyle thought, but he had a feeling he was going to be.

Very.

LATER THAT NIGHT, Amanda lay in bed wide-awake.

Everything had suddenly gotten out of control. Why had she agreed to the bet? What if she lost?

No, she reassured herself. She was good at what she did. She wouldn't lose. Besides, she had something more pressing to think about—the telephone call.

It had been from a New York television syndicate—Westec. They had seen the theme show she and Kyle had done and wanted her to fly to New York to talk with them about a job offer.

It had taken all her willpower to put it out of her mind while she'd had lunch with Kyle. It was probably the reason she'd agreed to his bet. She knew it was stupid, but she felt guilty that they'd made the offer to her alone. They'd made that quite clear.

It was a marvelous opportunity; a large promotion meaning more money and more prestige. It was everything she had been working toward.

So why did she feel so lousy?

8

AMANDA AND KYLE hardly saw each other in the days before the Oscar show.

In between sitting through every nominated movie again, Amanda sandwiched a quick one-day trip to New York. The New York television syndicate had given her two weeks to reach a decision about their job offer.

Kyle was busy shopping for his fantasy. He was going to take such pleasure in winning.

OSCAR NIGHT ARRIVED and with it Amanda's case of jitters. She decided she needed every advantage against Kyle to win the bet, so she pulled out all the stops. She would still wear her customary suit and pull her hair up, but with subtle differences a man would notice and hopefully be distracted by.

She took a long, relaxing soak in a herbal-scented bath to relax before she did her makeup. When she was satisfied with her face, she reached into the back of her closet and removed the outfit she planned to wear.

The tailored black suit had a side slit that flashed a sleek length of black-stockinged leg. Beneath the suit jacket she planned to wear a black satin camisole instead of a blouse. The same camisole she'd tried on in the dressing room when Kyle had been there. She wondered if he would remember and be distracted by the thought. She hoped so.

The small black hat she placed on her head was mostly veil. Wiping off her lip gloss, she slicked on red, red lipstick to accent her mouth below the sexy veil.

Diamond studs twinkled where her brown hair was swept behind her ears.

Sitting down on the bed, she added the final touch.... Her black leather three-inch heels showed a flash of toe cleavage, and her anklet lay seductively against her silken ankle.

She stood and glanced in the mirror for a final inspection and decided she looked decent enough to get past the censors, but her outfit definitely said celebration.

Picking up the small purse of black snakeskin containing the fantasy she'd written, she left for the studio.

KYLE SAUNTERED INTO the studio wearing a black tuxedo with a wing tip collar, playing his part to the hilt.

"Amanda here yet?" he asked Noah.

"Not yet," Noah answered. "You look like you're going to be getting some sort of award yourself tonight."

"One can only hope," Kyle said, chuckling to himself. He wondered which prim outfit Amanda would wear for the taping of the awards show. His lips creased into a wide grin when he thought of the purchases he made for her to fulfill his fantasy.

"Is that who I think it is?" Toby asked, his eyes wide.

Kyle turned and nearly choked when he saw Amanda. The delicate scalloped neckline of the black camisole lay against her pale skin, enhancing the luscious curve of her breasts.

Kyle ran his finger under the stiff white collar of his tuxedo shirt. He was in deep trouble. He wouldn't be able to remember his name much less his Oscar picks if he had to look at Amanda in that outfit on camera. He'd have to remember to keep his eyes off her as much as possible.

Right, and camels can fly, a voice in his head mocked as she walked toward him, the slit in her skirt baring a length of stockinged leg.

Amanda stopped to talk to Toby, giving Kyle a chance to regain his breath. He felt as if someone had punched him in his solar plexus. The lady didn't play fair at all. She'd purposely dressed to destroy his concentration.

Noah left to talk to the cameraman, and Kyle made his way over to where Amanda stood talking to Toby. One quelling glance from Kyle and the spellbound intern found somewhere else to be.

"Hi. Bring your envelope?" Kyle whispered, leaning in close so he wouldn't be overheard. It was a mistake, he realized, as a familiar scent teased his memory. He pulled back quickly to clear his head.

Amanda nodded and smiled smugly. "I hope you didn't bother to bring yours, as you won't be needing it."

"We'll see. . . ." Kyle countered, feigning a lazy confidence he didn't feel.

The excitement of the night already had Amanda feeling very giddy. Giddy enough to have worn the sexy outfit to exact a little advantage on Kyle.

Any advantage she had was negated by how smashing he looked in his tuxedo. He was a perfect example of a man wearing the clothes instead of the clothes wearing the man. No matter what he wore, Kyle was blatantly sexy and appealing. She glared at him in annoyance as the weatherman stopped to rub in last week's practical joke.

Kyle caught Amanda's look and knew he'd better win. He was half-afraid that when it came to him, her fantasy involved something unpleasant having to do with hot tar and feathers.

When the weatherman left, Kyle turned to Amanda. To lessen the tension between them, he nudged her playfully and nodded to the deserted hallway. "Come with me," he invited.

"No way," she answered, remembering all too well why he liked deserted hallways.

"I'll be good—promise," he said, stilling her objection by making a small cross over his heart.

She followed him into the hallway. "I don't really believe you brought your envelope," he teased.

"Well, I did."

"I'll show you mine if you'll show me yours," he said with a suggestive wink.

Deciding to humor him, she opened her small clutch and extracted a slim envelope, pale pink and a match to the three others she'd sent the fantasies to him in.

Kyle's eyes darkened and he swallowed the lump rising in his throat. Any doubts he might have harbored about her being his phantom correspondent vanished. She had definitely sent him the sexy fantasies.

When he recovered his composure, he turned playful again.

"I'm disappointed in you, Amanda."

"'Disappointed'?" she repeated, looking puzzled.

"Yeah, I've obviously worked much harder on my fantasy than you have on yours." Flashing her a drop-dead sexy grin, he slowly withdrew his envelope from his jacket pocket, comically removing the plain brown paper he'd wrapped around it for effect.

Amanda tried unsuccessfully to smother a smile at his antics, but her smile slid from her lips and her eyes widened when the envelope containing the fantasy he'd written came into view.

It was at least an inch thick!

"I was wondering where you'd gotten off to," Noah said, joining them in the hallway. "Well, are you two beautiful people ready to do the show?"

"Ye-yes," Amanda stammered, watching Kyle slip his thick envelope back into his tuxedo jacket with a pat.

"Well, then let's get the show in the can. Good luck to both of you."

"Thank the man," Kyle instructed Amanda. "You're going to need all the luck you can get, because I feel real lucky myself."

After a quick visit to makeup, they began taping.

Kyle's voice cracked halfway through his introduction to the show, when Amanda purposely crossed her legs and he caught a glimpse of the seams running up the backs of her black silk stockings.

They had to stop and restart the tape.

"Will you please behave yourself," Kyle whispered a bit desperately while the lighting director was making an adjustment to the lighting.

"But I'm at my best when I'm misbehaving," Amanda answered glibly, tossing his own words back to haunt him.

When they began retaping, Amanda almost missed her cue. She'd been so busy noticing how wonderful Kyle looked. He was all polish and shine from his black patent shoes to his gleaming baby blues. All the time he'd spent viewing movies had given him a flair for dressing up, or down, to any occasion. Not many men knew how to dress, and his effortless style was something Amanda really appreciated.

They had decided early on to concentrate on the top awards: best picture, song, director, actor, actress and supporting actor and actress.

The show got off to a slow start as they viewed and discussed film clips of the supporting players nominated. They had agreed on the same choices. An elderly actor was a sure win as a sentimental favorite, and a young English actress had made a smashing debut in a period piece the British were so fond of and excellent at producing.

It wasn't until they got around to the songs nominated for an Oscar that the fireworks started between them.

Kyle's choice was a song written and performed by a rock star who had scored the entire movie. The song had made it to the top of the pop charts, as had the sound track from the film.

"A rock star?" Amanda mocked upon hearing his voice. "Really, Kyle."

"Sure, why not?"

"You can't be serious," Amanda questioned, enjoying putting him on the defensive, although she was pleased with his choice. A rock star winning an Oscar was a long shot at best.

"Ah, but not just any rock star," Kyle said by way of defending his choice. "This one went to Juilliard."

Amanda shot him a pained expression. "That doesn't mean anything, except that his parents had the money to send him."

"He went on scholarship," Kyle answered smugly.

"Ah, but did he stay?" Amanda quipped, hurrying on to her choice for best song. She picked the popular instrumental by a brilliant composer. It was from a film that had been a critical success but had done poorly at the box office.

"You chose *that* drivel? I should have known you'd be a sucker for romantic pap after you picked *Doctor Zhivago* on the other show. Sorry, but you lose on this one."

"I hardly think so," Amanda said in her best snooty tone. "It's the sign of a good song when it stays in your head, playing over and over."

Kyle snorted. "If you ask me, that's the sign of an annoying commercial."

Amanda sighed. "Since you obviously have no taste in music, I think we should move on to the next nomination." She nodded to signal the next film clip.

"Now wait just a minute," Kyle said, waving off the film clip. "What do you mean I have no taste in music? I suppose you're an expert?"

"At least I listen to something besides rock and roll. Do you have any albums from before the sixties?"

"No, but—"

"I rest my case."

The film clips came up for best director.

"I'd like to arrest your case, handcuffs and all," Kyle whispered in frustration off camera.

"Handcuffs?" Amanda repeated, raising an eyebrow beneath the netted veil covering one side of her forehead. "Anything else?"

Kyle shot her a dark look. "A gag would be nice...."

Back on camera, Amanda picked a foreign director for an epic film.

"This is a close call," Kyle ventured, hating to have to agree with her choice. "It could go with the action/adventure picture, but I respect what the director of the epic tried to do, so I'm going with him, too," he confirmed grudgingly.

Noah, watching, was delighted with the way the show was playing. Amanda and Kyle struck sparks off each other professionally as well as physically. Where Amanda was analytical, Kyle was a seat-of-the-pants performer. Where Amanda was substance, Kyle was charm. They complemented each other, and both were very good.

The film clips for best actor ran, and Kyle went first with his choice.

"This is another close call, but I'm going to go against type. James Warson isn't typical leading-man material, but he takes chances. He has a good body of work behind him, and I think the academy will recognize that this year."

"I agree," Amanda said.

"You agree? Just like that? No argument for Mr. Heartthrob?"

"No," Amanda answered, pursing her lips with sweet innocence.

Kyle's eyes narrowed at the provocative red lipstick she wore. He wasn't sure which made him crazier—the aloof Amanda or the seductive Amanda. His hands were measuring her throat again, and he knew where thoughts of his hands on her body led.... His eyes strayed to the silky camisole.

"Okay." He took a deep, calming breath. "Let's proceed to the best actress category, then," he said, nodding for the film clips.

This time they hardly agreed.

"Well," Amanda began, "there's no question but that Marcia Adams will win another Oscar for her outstanding performance."

"Give me a break." Kyle sighed. "Marcia Adams's mantel won't hold another Oscar. Anyway, this time she's not even in the running with Traci Marselli. Her twisted hooker roll in the psychological thriller steamed right off the screen."

"Hookers are easy to play," Amanda said, rejecting his assessment. "All you need is a good body, lingerie and a voyeur cinematographer."

"Sounds like Venus envy to me," Kyle said, looking at his fingernails.

Amanda's mouth dropped open.

Kyle nodded for the clips for the award for best picture.

"'Venus envy'?" Amanda repeated off camera.

Kyle made an attempt to look ashamed but broke up with laughter, instead.

Amanda eyed him without indulgence.

"Okay, I'm sorry," he said, throwing up his palms in surrender. "I can't resist a bad pun. Actually, it's my evil twin who can't. Did I ever tell you about him?"

He didn't get a chance to. They were back on camera.

It was a foregone conclusion by both the public and the press that a popular movie would win.

Predictably, Amanda chose that picture.

Kyle, on the other hand, amazed Amanda by picking another movie out of left field.

"What?" she asked in openmouthed amazement. The cameraman zoomed in for a close-up of her reaction. "If that movie wins, I'll . . . I'll . . ."

"Want me to tell them what you'll do?" Kyle covered his mike as he whispered off camera, patting the envelope in his tuxedo jacket with a wicked wink.

"I'll . . . I'll," she stammered. "I'll iron your shirts for a week," she said hastily into the camera.

"Cut," Noah called. "That's a wrap. Good show, you two."

"Iron my shirts for a week?" Kyle repeated incredulously as he took off his microphone. "I'll have to check," he said, pulling the envelope from his tuxedo jacket, "but I don't think I have anything in here about your ironing my shirts."

"I had to say *something*," Amanda replied as Kyle slipped the envelope back into his jacket pocket.

"That's okay," he assured her, standing up. "We'll consider it an added bonus I get when I win tonight."

She glared at him and stood, too.

He chuckled. "And you can't renege. I've got you on tape."

"That's the only place you've got me," she retorted, taking off her microphone. "With that last choice, you assured I'd win the bet."

"No way. You're gonna lose your sweet little behind . . . baby," he said, swatting her playfully.

"Fine," Amanda said, giving as good as she got. "If I should lose, I'll iron your shirts . . . with you in them."

"Whoa . . . the lady is into S and M," Kyle said, making a vampire cross in front of him and backing away, his eyes wide with pretended alarm. "Maybe I ought to reconsider this fantasy business."

"Maybe you ought," she answered, striking a provocative pose.

"Nah . . . you're just toying with me," he decided. "And that's all right." He wriggled his eyebrows lasciviously. "I've always wanted to be a boy toy."

Amanda gave an exaggerated sigh.

She had a feeling it was going to be a long night.

Her only consoling thought was of winning. She'd made safe choices against Kyle's wild card picks. Sure, there would be a fluke award or two—there always was. But safety was the sure bet.

And when she won, there was no way Kyle would do the fantasy she'd perversely written on the pale pink stationery in the envelope in her purse.

She'd be off the hook . . . and cured of taking dares forever.

She hoped.

"GOT ANY POPCORN?" Kyle asked, loosening his tuxedo tie with his long fingers while Amanda unlocked the door to the carriage house.

"Microwave," she answered, nodding to the galley kitchen when they were inside.

While he went in search of the popcorn, she set her purse on the desk and walked over to switch on the television in the armoire. The final credits of *The Barbara Walters Special* were crawling up the screen, which meant the Academy Awards were due to start. It would be at least another hour until they got around to handing out the top awards. Knowing that did nothing for her case of increasingly jittery nerves.

She lifted off her tiny black hat, her shaking hands snagging the veil on a loose hairpin. After working the veil free, she smoothed the loose tendrils back into her sleek chignon, her eyes lingering on the poof of hat in her hand.

She was pleased the provocative outfit had the unsettling effect on Kyle she'd intended. Unfortunately, it was now having an unsettling effect on her. The sexy trappings of femininity reminded her of something she knew all too well. The attraction between them was man/woman and purely physical.

At least it was on Kyle's part. It was her bad luck to have fallen in love with a man who wasn't the sort to spend the rest of his life with any *one* woman.

She set her hat down with a sigh. Behind her, the cabinet doors stopped banging open and closed. Kyle had found the cabinet where she stored the popcorn.

"I'll cook if you do drinks," he called, setting the timer on the microwave for three minutes.

"Sounds fair," Amanda said, joining him. Opening the refrigerator, she withdrew two cans of cola and popped the tabs.

"What, no wine?" Kyle teased in genial banter.

"I'm out of wine. Besides," she said, shooting him a knowing look, "wine is what got me into this impossible position to begin with."

An impish grin tugged the corners of Kyle's lips as he rubbed the cleft in his squared chin. There was laughter in the eyes that roved over her in delicious sexual speculation. He couldn't resist. "Wine gets you into impossible positions. . . . Really? Excuse me. I'll just be a minute while I run up to the liquor store."

A pained expression crossed Amanda's pretty features.

Kyle tried an unsuccessful look of repentance, then threw up his palms in surrender. "It wasn't me. Truly. It was my evil twin. . . . Have I mentioned him?"

A furious round of popping ended with the pinging sound of the microwave timer, and he turned to retrieve the popcorn.

"Wait a minute," he said, turning back to Amanda, and handing her the bag of popcorn. He rested his fingertips on his lean hips, the stance as provocative in tuxedo pants as in frayed, faded jeans. "Are you claiming I got you drunk at lunch last week and then took unfair advantage, getting you to agree to this dare?" he demanded, his eyes narrowed.

Amanda shook the warm, buttery popcorn into a bowl. The aroma mingled with his mossy after-shave, triggering Amanda's erotic memories of sharing popcorn with him the first time they'd reviewed a film together.

She nibbled her bottom lip hesitantly.

"Amanda..."

"Okay, so I've got this bad habit of being unable to turn down a dare, wine or no wine. Are you happy now?" she huffed, crossing her arms in front of her.

Kyle picked up a fistful of popcorn and scrunched it into his mouth as he considered her. "Suppose I dare you to take off all your clothes?"

She looked at him as though he were a specimen under a microscope.

"Okay, okay. So how come you can't turn down a dare, anyway?"

She shrugged. "I don't know. I guess it's my stubborn nature."

"So you *do* admit you're stubborn."

"Sure. The same as you."

"*I'm* not stubborn," he objected.

"Right, you're not stubborn," she mocked, rolling her eyes ceilingward.

"I'm not."

"You refused to even give me the benefit of the doubt when Noah hired me to be your cohost," she pointed out by way of example.

"That's not stubborn," he said, holding his ground with tenacity.

"Oh, it's not? What do you call it, then?" she asked, taking a swallow of cola.

"Smart," he said, pitching a kernel of popcorn up in the air and catching it with his mouth. His twinkling blue eyes made an obvious journey over her body, slowing at the appropriate curves. "One look at you and I couldn't remember my name. How could I expect anyone else to?"

She shook her head at his ploy of flattery, not believing for a moment that he was sincere. "Okay, I give in. You're right. You're not stubborn. You're a prince." With that, she picked up the bowl of popcorn and headed for the love seat in front of the television.

Kyle's lusty laugh followed her all the way. He grabbed the two cans of cola and trailed after her. "I'm no prince any more than you're the ice princess you pretend." Setting down the cans of cola on the glass coffee table, he dropped beside her onto the love seat and made himself comfortable. He regarded her through eyes lowered to a sexy half-mast, his thumb rubbing back and forth across his lower lip. "You really are bad, you know, sending me those anonymous fantasies...."

For the first time, Amanda was sorry she'd bought the soft, cushy love seat. It was much too inviting.

He was much too inviting. He was much too close. And she was much too vulnerable to his cocky charm and the love words that fell so easily from his lips.

Reaching for her feet, he unnerved her even further, pulling them up to rest on his hard thighs.

She watched him warily as he slipped off her high heels and tossed them back over the love seat carelessly.

"Why did you do it?" he asked huskily, his talented hands beginning to stroke and squeeze her stockinged feet by turn.

"Why do you think?" she snapped, avoiding his eyes and trying to wriggle free from hands that were massaging her into sensual Nirvana.

His eyes flicked up to hers. "I think you did it because you want me as much as I want you," he challenged.

She managed to twist her feet from his grasp. "I *did* it to get back at you," she said, tucking her feet beneath her.

"To get back at me. What did I do?"

"What did you do! You fought having me for your cohost every inch of the way."

He refused to rise to her bait. "I didn't do anything different than you would have if our situation had been reversed."

His words stopped her. He'd said them with complete conviction. For him it was professional competition, nothing personal. *Had* she been kidding herself? Was what he said the truth?

Kyle grabbed a handful of popcorn and wedged the bowl between his thighs. "Go ahead. Don't be shy. Help yourself to a handful whenever you want," he offered, teasing her out of her silence.

She shot him a schoolteacher look of reprimand.

"All right, okay," he said, returning the bowl of popcorn to the coffee table in front of them. "But you can't blame a guy for trying." His smile was sly and wicked. "As I remember, I really like how your reach doesn't exceed your...ah...grasp. Any possibility your fantasy involves popcorn?" he asked. "You know, on the slim chance you might win tonight."

"No popcorn."

"No?"

"No."

He tossed a few kernels into his mouth and thought a moment. "Butter?" he asked hopefully, a seductive glint in his eyes.

Amanda just looked at him.

"Guess not, huh?" he said, slipping out of his tuxedo jacket and tossing it aside. He rolled up his shirtsleeves, waiting.

"Right," he said finally when she didn't answer him.

They managed to devour the popcorn by the time the lesser awards were handed out.

The Oscar currently being announced was for best supporting actor. Their choice for best supporting actress won earlier in the show. They were in a one-to-one tie, and this award wouldn't break it since they'd both picked the same supporting actor to win.

When the winner was announced, they were both right again, and the score between them was still a tie.

"Now we're getting down to the real nitty-gritty," Kyle said, rubbing his hands together enthusiastically. The best actress award was to be announced after the upcoming commercial.

"Can I put my feet up?" he asked, removing his patent loafers and moving the empty popcorn bowl from the coffee table to the floor.

"Sure. Make yourself comfortable," Amanda answered, regretting her words a second later when he did just that, sliding his arm around her shoulders and drawing her into the curve of his arm.

"What do you think you're doing?"

"Pretending we're in the balcony," he answered with an incorrigible smile.

"Is that where you got interested in movies?"

"It's where I got interested in a lot of things."

She tore her gaze away from the invitation in his eyes and made a pretense of being interested in which detergent got her clothes cleanest. The awards came back on, and Kyle's attention also returned to the television screen.

"This is where you start losing," he promised.

"Dream on. There's no way that sex kitten is going to win an award."

Kyle shrugged. "Depends on how many men are in the academy."

"*Some* men have taste."

"I'd rather have a libido."

"I don't think you have to worry."

"Yeah, I know. I've got both."

He was right, of course. About everything. The sex kitten won.

Kyle chuckled as Amanda's bottom lip puckered into a barely detectable and very delectable pout.

Reaching over, he trailed his finger along the curve of her jaw. "Well, it looks like it's going to be my night, doesn't it? Let's see now, I'll be needing silk scarves . . ."
He leaned in to nibble at her provocative bottom lip.

"*Four* of them," he whispered, sending goose bumps across her shoulders.

"I only have two," Amanda lied, pretending innocence.

"Well, we'll just have to improvise, then, won't we?" he said, trailing his finger along the edge of her slit skirt and over her stockinged leg.

"But you haven't won yet," she said, pushing his hand away and forcing herself to pull back from the warm, sultry atmosphere his nearness created.

"But I will," he promised. "The gods are with me tonight. I'm planning ahead, is all."

"Then plan on going home, because you're going to lose."

"Amanda, sweet. You're simply not paying attention. I'm already in the lead."

"But it's not over—"

"Till it's over. I know. But what about this feeling I've got in my gut that this thing between us is never going to be over?" he murmured.

Amanda looked away. He knew all the right words to say. If only he meant them. But, of course, he didn't. Men like him never did. How did women resist men who were so devastatingly handsome, charming and sexy?

She knew the answer: they didn't.

And lived to regret it, she warned herself. Still, if she went into this with her eyes wide open . . .

The next award was up, and their attention returned to the television screen, the score between them three to two, with Kyle in the lead.

The Oscar was for best director, and they both lost as the academy picked the director of the popular action/adventure film nominated.

"Getting nervous yet?" Kyle asked, not bothering to hide his delight at still being in the lead. He got up and headed for the galley kitchen.

"What are you doing?" she called, turning to look over her shoulder.

Kyle stood with his hands braced on his knees, peering inside her refrigerator. "Just checking," was his muffled reply. As she watched he shifted his weight to one foot, stretching the sleek tuxedo pants snug over his tight buttocks.

She turned back around, covered her eyes with her hands and shook her head.

Moments later he returned empty-handed and sat back down beside her.

"You're out of whipped cream," he said with a sexy wink.

"You're a crazy man."

He arched an eyebrow. "And who made me crazy, sending me those hot letters?" he asked, running his fingertip along the scalloped edge of her black satin camisole. "And crazier still when I found out it was you," he growled.

"Will you *please* forget about those letters," she said through gritted teeth, pushing his hand away.

"Make me," he dared, his voice low and wickedly suggestive as the next Oscar was announced for presentation. It was the Oscar for best actor. Since they had agreed with each other on a nominee, it didn't affect the score they were keeping between them. This time their pick was on target, and the score remained in Kyle's favor, four to three.

Amanda glanced over at him after the announcement.

He showed no mercy. "So. Got anything in leather?" he purred, running his hands through his shaggy blond hair as he stretched. The action pulled open one of the studs on his tuxedo shirt.

She ignored his question and tried not to drool.

He wouldn't let it drop. "Minis, thigh-high boots, whips . . ."

She swallowed and looked away. No wonder his fantasy was an inch thick!

He ran his finger along the table backing the love seat and got her attention when he brought his fingertip close to his eyes for inspection. He shook his head sorrowfully at the dust he'd collected.

"Tsk, tsk," he clucked. "You obviously don't own a feather duster. Now if you did, I could show you things . . ."

A trickle of perspiration slithered between Amanda's breasts.

"That's okay," he said with the good humor of someone with a winning hand. "I like to shop. I can pick up the feather duster when I get the whipped cream and . . . other things."

"I'm going to scream," Amanda muttered under her breath.

Kyle leaned close, tipping her chin with his dusty forefinger. Smiling wickedly into her eyes, he said, "Count on it."

His words were like putting a match to kindling, igniting the passion seething inside her. Frightened by how easily Kyle could intoxicate her with his love words, Amanda returned her attention to the television screen as an actress famous for her outrageous style as much as for her acting began the presentation of the Oscar for best song.

Amanda's palms began to sweat.

She held her breath. On this one she'd gone against her own tastes. She liked the rock-and-roll sound track from the movie Kyle had picked, but she didn't think the older members of the academy would vote for it.

They didn't. Her pick won the Oscar for best song.

As she leaped up enthusiastically and applauded their choice, Kyle remained seated, appreciating the soft bounce of her breasts, obviously unrestrained beneath her sexy black camisole.

"Now look who's feeling cocky," Kyle said, laughing up at the smug look of triumph shining on her face.

"You lose, Kyle," she promised, looking down at him. "There's no way you can win now. Not with that off-the-wall pick you made for best picture."

"It's not over till—" he began, mocking her with her own words.

"Oh, it's over," she said, interrupting him. "I might as well start boiling the tar right now."

"Tar!" Kyle's eyes widened in a pretense of alarm. "Have mercy, woman," he begged, sliding from the love seat to his knees before her.

"I did. I tore up the fantasy I wrote about having you drawn and quartered," she said, smiling down on him with exaggerated sweetness.

She became aware immediately that Kyle was not at any disadvantage being on his knees before her.

Tilting her hips forward gently with his hands, he nuzzled her belly with his chin and gazed up at her with a seductive gleam in his eyes.

"Whatever happened to those other fantasies you used to have about me, Amanda? I liked them ever so much better."

Desire, hot and urgent, spiraled upward from where Kyle's chin rested on her belly. Coherent thought became impossible. "Uh . . ."

"Want to call it a tie and break off the bet before you lose?" he offered, his voice amused and husky.

As she looked down at him, she gave his offer serious consideration. In the end her stubbornness prevailed.

"No. I always keep my bargains. Besides—" she tossed her head regally "—I'm going to win."

"But you might not," Kyle said, rising to his feet.

"I'll take my chances," she said, lifting her chin.

He laughed at her show of defiance. "Aren't you going to offer me the same bargain I made you?"

"Is that what you want?"

His laugh was low and wicked as he pulled her down beside him on the love seat. "You know what I want."

She bit her lip, then expelled her breath when she saw that the commercials were over and the film clips of the nominees for best picture were flashing on the screen.

They both watched as the star of the year's hit musical announced the nominees and took her own sweet time slitting open the envelope containing the winner.

Amanda and Kyle couldn't have been any more keyed up if they'd been in a nominated film.

Against all odds, Kyle's off-the-wall pick won.

Amanda couldn't believe her ears. Kyle had won the contest on a fluke! The score between them ended at five to four in Kyle's favor.

"Ahem. . . ."

She turned to the sound of Kyle clearing his throat mischievously.

His slow grin was lethal as their eyes met.

"I believe," he drawled, "this is where you say, 'The envelope, please.'"

9

Amanda eyed the thick envelope Kyle withdrew from the pocket of the tuxedo jacket he'd discarded on the love seat.

"There's nothing illegal in your fantasy, is there?" she asked, searching for a way out.

Kyle laughed. "Probably, in some states. If that's a problem, I'm not above taking you across the state line," he promised with an unrepentant wink as he reached for her.

"I think I'd better read it first," she said, staving him off as she snatched the envelope from his hand.

"Uh-uh," Kyle said, taking the envelope back. "I think you'd better kiss me first."

Amanda's eyes narrowed as she assessed him suspiciously. "How do I know there's kissing in your fantasy unless I read it?"

"Oh, it's in there," Kyle assured her. Twirling an imaginary villain's mustache, he lowered his voice to a cautionary whisper. "Kissing and *worse*."

"Worse?"

"Okay, better," he breathed, his lips brushing hers sensually, urging them to open to him.

Her eyes fluttered closed as he leaned her back against the arm of the love seat, discarding the envelope on the coffee table.

Their bodies made full contact as his tongue slipped into the warm, moist recesses of her mouth. Delicious shivers swept through her, intensified by the ritual of thrust and parry. He pulled back from her lips for breath, his mouth open, his teeth raking delicately over her jaw and down the tender flesh of her throat. His hands slipped beneath her hips, pulling her up to meet the hard evidence of his arousal. He ground his hips against hers once, then flung himself away from her on a tortured groan.

"No. This is all going too fast," he said, trying to regain control of his raging passion. When his breathing returned to normal, he looked down at his watch. "It's already almost midnight. I think it's only fair that we reschedule this for tomorrow night, say around seven?"

How could he stop! Amanda wanted to kill him. Slowly. She didn't want to stop. What she wanted was for the wondering, the dancing around each other, the sexual tension between them—the torture—to stop.

That would only happen if they made love.

"Promise me you won't look at my fantasy until you're in the bath tomorrow right before I arrive," he said, ignoring her pique as he slipped on his shoes and shrugged on his jacket.

Amanda nodded reluctantly, willing him to just leave.

He provoked her further by kissing her lightly on the nose and saying, "I still have to shop, remember?"

As he left, it was clear to Amanda that this was just a game to him. He intended to savor his victory, nothing more.

She gathered up the empty cola cans and popcorn bowl, carrying them to the kitchen after switching off the TV.

Her anger simmered as she rinsed the bowl, and she let the job offer from the New York syndicate seep into her thoughts. It was only fair that she tell Kyle. Still, she hadn't been entirely certain she would until now. His little stunt tonight had made up her mind. Even if she didn't take the job, she wanted him to know about the offer. She would tell him, all right. *After* she'd honored their bet.

She hadn't made up her mind one way or the other about the offer, and time was growing short. By the end of next week she'd need to give Westec her decision. A decision she was no closer to having made than the day they'd offered her the job.

What would Kyle's reaction be when she told him? she wondered. Would he tell her to take the job or ask her to stay? What would he do in her position? Would he give up a job opportunity, a break like working for the New York syndicate, if it was him being offered the job instead of her?

She didn't want to think about the answer to that question. She was afraid she already knew it.

He wouldn't be in the same quandary she was in, because he didn't feel about her the way she felt about him. But what if he did? Would a man give up a job opportunity in favor of a relationship with a woman who meant more to him?

Probably not, she concluded, turning out the lights.

AMANDA DECIDED she hated Kyle Fox's guts.

It had been bad enough that he'd won the bet between them. But then he'd suggested they wait a night, the rat. Surely he'd known by now she'd become the basket case she was.

And what was he really shopping for? No, she didn't even want to think about that.

Her hand shook as she tore open the dainty envelope of perfumed bath salts she'd bought at a little boutique next to the cinema at the mall. After emptying the envelope beneath the spigot splashing steamy water into the tub, she removed the wrapper from a small bar of soap in a matching fragrance.

Taking a deep breath, she let her satin robe slide from her smooth, pale shoulders to the cool tile floor. Goose bumps rose on her bare skin as her body quivered in nervous anticipation of Kyle's arrival for the culmination of their bet. Setting the new bar of soap in the soap dish, she stepped into the tub of warm, sudsy water, reaching for her bath pillow.

Her head rested against the soft pillow as she slid farther down into the soothing froth of bubbly water. Moving her hands absently, she lapped the fragrant water over herself in sensual waves, thinking back to the night before and Kyle's wicked smile when he'd pulled out the envelope containing his fantasy.

She'd kept her promise not to read it, but it hadn't been the easiest thing she'd ever done. Over and over she'd been tempted to open the envelope, picking it up and putting it back down again and again. In the end, she'd decided she would be much better off not knowing what Kyle wanted until right before he arrived.

Glancing over at her watch lying on the vanity, she saw that it was six o'clock. She had an hour to read his fantasy and get ready before he was due to arrive.

The still-sealed envelope sat on the edge of the tub like a ticking time bomb.

She reached for it.

When she'd agreed to Kyle's dare of acting out his fantasy, she'd never dreamed she'd lose the bet. The emotions she felt after losing were mixed, running the gamut from shy embarrassment to anxious trepidation to wanton excitement.

All sorts of erotic images flashed in her mind as possibilities when she slipped her long fingernail under the flap of the envelope to open it.

Withdrawing the contents, she saw there was something inside besides stationery to account for it's thickness. The yellow legal paper containing his fantasy was wrapped around several layers of slick pink gift tissue.

Setting the fantasy aside for a moment, she unfolded the tissue, uttering a small gasp of delight when she saw what it contained. A string of tiny diamond chips twinkled in an exquisite gold anklet.

She couldn't keep it, of course, but she was too much of a woman not to try it on. Impulsively, she lifted her foot from the water, bending her leg at the knee. When she had the anklet fastened, she raised her leg high in the air to admire Kyle's gift. Pale pink polish on her toes peeked out from dollops of suds as the soapy water sluiced down her leg.

Resting her leg on the spigot, she admired the anklet's sparkle as she turned her foot this way and that.

Then she picked up the yellow legal paper covered with Kyle's bold scrawl and began reading.

Amanda, sweet,

I'm picturing you now as you lie back in a tub of warm, soapy water, trailing a slippery sponge over your body. The room is fragrant and steamy, lulling you into sensual lassitude as you admire the diamond trinket twinkling on your delicate ankle. You have tried it on, haven't you?

The anklet is all I want you wearing when I come for you, except perhaps a robe when you open the door to me.

While you wait, lie back and let me entertain you with fleeting images. . . .

It's winter. Listen to the wind howling across the frozen field and through the barren trees. I can just see you now, coming through the clearing.

You look so snug and warm with that fur lap robe tucked around you as you drive your pretty two-horse carriage down the road.

You turn suddenly at the whinny of my horse. You do see me, don't you? Sitting astride my black stallion at the crest of the hill.

I'm wearing a long, black coat and a black Stetson. See the frosty breath of my horse as he stamps impatiently, anxious to be off. Watch as I rein him in and turn to descend the hill.

Are you going to follow me down to the other side of the hill? You will, if you're the woman I think you are.

Don't be startled because you don't see me at first, only my horse grazing on a patch of scrub grass. I'm over by the big tree in a fur-lined sleeping bag that's half-unzipped. Enough so that you can see I'm naked, my body hair running rampant over my hard chest and lower still.

Don't you want to join me, Amanda? Or perhaps you'd prefer a warmer setting. . . .

In that case, it's summer now. The air is hot and still. Nothing moves save the ceiling fan circling lazily over your bed. The air in the room is hot and stifling.

As you toss and turn restlessly beneath the mosquito netting canopied over your bed, your thin, white cotton gown clings damply to your thighs.

Unable to sleep, you go down to the parlor for a mint julep and stand sipping it in the dark. The glass is cool and wet as you rub it across your flushed cheek.

Suddenly you hear a noise outside the window. You look out through the space between the gauzy curtains fluttering listlessly on a stray, feeble breeze.

Do you see me silhouetted in the flare of the match I've just struck to light my cheroot? I'm slouched against the veranda railing, shirtless and shoeless. I can't sleep, either, but it's not the heat that's bothering me.

My bare chest is sweat slicked, and as you watch, a trickle of sweat slides down to my belly. Your eyes lin-

*ger, noticing how the faded jeans I'm wearing outline
my sex. It's plain that I'm aroused. The pupils of your
eyes grow soft and wide as you also notice my jeans are
unsnapped. Looking up, you see I'm watching you.*

Will you respond to the dare in my eyes . . . ?

Amanda's eyes drifted closed and the yellow paper
in her hand slipped into the water as she became lost in
the fantasy.

Moments later her eyes were jerked open by the insistent appeal of her doorbell. Her gaze flew to her
watch on the vanity. It was only six-thirty. Kyle wasn't
due to arrive until seven.

The rat! He'd purposely timed it so he would catch
her in her bath. That was his reason for wanting her to
wait to read his fantasy. Now she had no choice but to
open the door to him wearing nothing but her robe and
the glittery anklet, as he'd wanted.

How long had he been ringing the doorbell? she
wondered as she dried off quickly and pulled on her
satin robe.

"Amanda, sweet," she heard him calling as she hurried to answer her door. "Let me in or I'll huff and I'll
puff and I'll blow—"

She pulled open the door.

Kyle was standing there laden with packages. She
recognized the hem of his white denim cowboy duster
and the silver-tipped boots he'd been wearing when
she'd first met him.

"What's all this?" she asked as he staggered in the door, trying to keep the packages on top of the stack from their sideways slide.

A muffled response came from behind the pile.

Amanda reached to remove the top packages hiding Kyle's face.

"Told you I was going shopping," he said with a wink.

"But . . ."

The look in his eyes stopped her protest as his blue gaze raked over her disheveled appearance. Her top-knot was half-undone, its dark tendrils clinging to the still-damp skin at her throat. The beginnings of a smile tugged at his lips as he sought out her right ankle.

The diamond anklet he'd given her glittered there, matching the satisfaction glittering in his eyes. "Good." He nodded. "I see you followed my directions."

"As if I had a choice. . . . You had this all planned out to the second, didn't you?"

He gave her the point, looking very pleased with himself. "Planning is what separates the men from the boys."

"Is it?" she commented, studying him and the packages while he stood before her grinning ear to ear.

"What is all this?" she asked, not sure she wanted to know.

"Come with me and find out," he answered over his shoulder, climbing the steps to her bedroom."

"I'm waiting. . . ." he called down when she didn't immediately follow him up the stairs.

"Amanda Butterworth, you are never, *ever* taking another dare as long as you live, do you hear me?" she admonished herself under her breath as she stood at the bottom of the stairs contemplating what taking this dare had gotten her into.

"A-man-da...."

"Okay, okay. I'm coming. Keep your pants on," she muttered, then giggled nervously, realizing the inaneness of what she'd said. Taking a deep breath, she began the slow climb up the stairs to her bedroom, where he waited.

She saw him when she reached the top of the stairs.

He sat on her bed as though he belonged there. His long legs were crossed carelessly at his booted ankles, and his back was braced against her brass headboard. The packages he'd brought were scattered on the bed at his feet.

When she hesitated, his eyes narrowed.

She approached the bed and added the two packages in her hands to the pile at his feet, then moved away.

Gone was the teasing man she'd opened the door to. In his place was a silent, watchful one. One who looked rather dangerous, she thought, her heartbeat speeding up.

"Undo your robe," he said quietly.

"What's in these packages?" she asked by way of diversion, moving to open the closest one.

"Undo your robe," he repeated with quiet authority.

"Close your eyes," she answered impetuously, stepping back from the bed.

He shook his head. "Uh-uh. I want to watch. That's what this is all about."

"That's your fantasy?"

He nodded. "Get dressed in the things I've bought you, and I'll take you someplace special."

"That's all? You just want to watch me dress?"

He nodded.

She considered him. He didn't smile. No flirtatious wink. Nothing.

"Undo the robe."

Biting her lip, she lifted her hands to untie the belt cinching the waist of her pink satin robe.

"Move." He motioned, positioning her in front of the large mirror over her dressing table. She stood facing him, her back reflected in the mirror, as she waited for his next instruction.

"Shrug and let the robe fall."

The robe whispered to the floor, leaving her naked before him.

"You're very beautiful," he whispered hoarsely. In no other way did he react to her nakedness. His eyes only left her once, flickering briefly to her reflection in the mirror.

He nodded to the pile of packages at his feet. She looked down and back at him. His eyes locked with hers.

"Now get dressed," he instructed. "I want you to take your time. Pretend I'm not even in the room. You're alone, understand?" he asked, his voice sensual and compelling.

She nodded, her eyes soft and wide.

He waited.

The silence in the room was deafening.

She walked to the bed and began opening the packages scattered by his booted feet.

To her surprise, there wasn't a single scrap of black lace or leather. In fact, quite the opposite. Each item she withdrew from the pastel tissue in gift-wrapped boxes was frilly, demure and white.

And each item would fit, she was sure. Kyle Fox was the kind of man who would know how to gauge a woman's size with his practiced eye. It was a knowledge that didn't annoy her. There was something endearing about a man who enjoyed looking at a woman, enjoyed buying her pretty things enough to develop a discerning taste and style.

Picking up a flat, slim box, she unwrapped the tissue from an eyelet-and-ribbon-trimmed garter belt and a pair of pale silk stockings and entered Kyle's fantasy.

His fantasy didn't surprise her. He wanted to watch her perform an intimate ritual for him. His participation would be from a distance, allowing him to maintain the aloofness he so valued...allowing him to keep his feelings hidden. They weren't so different, he and she.

As Kyle had instructed, Amanda pretended to be alone, but every move she made was designed to pleasure him. She meant to arouse him, to give him something better than any fantasy. If she did indeed go to New York, she wasn't going to be so easy to forget.

Instinctively she played to the mirror above her dressing table as Kyle sat fully clothed on her bed watching her. The contrast of his clothing with her nakedness excited her.

Every fiber of her being tingled with the thrill of doing something forbidden. Every inch of her flesh felt him watching her. She shivered and a faint flush crept over her pale skin as she fastened the tiny hooks and eyes of the garter belt.

Taking a seat on the plush vanity bench before her dressing table, she raised one shapely leg, bending it at the knee. Bunching one pale stocking in her fingertips, she slipped the puddle of silk over her prettily arched foot, being careful not to snag the sheer stocking on the slim circlet of flat diamond chain lying against her ankle.

Then, straightening her leg above her head with the grace of a dancer, she eased the filmy silk up the contours of her sleek calf, over her knee and on up until the top of the stocking rested snugly on her firm thigh. Placing a hand on either side of her ankle, she smoothed the silk with deliberate leisure up her leg again, tugging the stocking top to secure it.

She followed suit with the other stocking, all the while feeling the warmth of Kyle's gaze on her. Posing made her feel as lascivious as a centerfold model, except Kyle's eyes were the camera recording her every move.

Her cheeks felt feverish and her hands trembled slightly as she caught a glimpse of Kyle's heavy-lidded gaze in the mirror. She steeled herself to ignore him as he'd requested.

When she stood, her fingertips barely grazed the tops of her stockings. She watched herself in the mirror while she adjusted the eyelet-and-ribbon-trimmed garters caressing the stockings on her sleek thighs.

Pivoting slowly to face the bed, she turned her head over her shoulder, then stood high on tiptoe tilting her softly rounded hips slightly forward so she could check her reflection in the mirror.

To keep her balance, she braced her hands on her hips, the resulting arch of her back thrusting her pretty breasts even higher. As she tried to check the backs of her stockings, her toes wavered slightly in the difficult pose.

Finally, satisfied that her stockings were straight, she went down from her toes and reached to pick up the shoe box on the bed. Opening it, she found a pair of old-fashioned white kid boots beneath the tissue. It was a style that was once again trendy. The dainty boots had two-inch heels and laced up to the ankle.

Dropping them to the floor before her, she toed her feet into the soft boots inch by inch until she worked them on. Then, with her profile to the bed, she placed one booted foot up on the plush vanity bench. When she leaned down to lace up the boot, her full, upturned breasts swung forward, grazing the tender inside of her arms. Her already puckered nipples pebbled instantly into hard arousal. She gave out a little gasp at the corresponding tightening in her groin and the moistness gathering there, then forced herself to concentrate on finishing lacing the boots.

Behind her she heard Kyle take a deep breath when she unstopped the bottle of Pleasure perfume on her dressing table and began trailing the fragrant glass stopper between her breasts and just above the patch of soft fuzz between her legs. The heavy, sensual scent she'd sprinkled over the letters she'd written Kyle wafted around the room, triggering erotically charged images from those fantasies . . . and the ones he'd written her on the yellow legal paper. Intimate images shared only by the two of them. A special secret they shared, bonding them together as one.

She smiled with her eyes as she leaned forward to pick up a tube of shiny pink lip gloss from the tray on her dressing table, puckering her lips into a provocative pout to apply it. The look she gave the mirror was sultry and inviting.

A bedspring squeaked as Kyle shifted his weight. Still he didn't get up, continuing instead to sit and watch.

Suddenly it was a challenge to get him to react to her. Her promise of never, *ever* taking another dare was forgotten.

Turning, she picked up the white box from the bed, recognizing the embossed signature on top. It was from an exclusive shop. Inside was a silk charmeuse camisole trimmed with Versailles lace.

Moving back to the mirror, she raised her arms above her head and slipped the narrow shoulder straps on. The filmy camisole fluttered down to settle over her breasts, the shadow of her nipples poking at the fabric with slinky temptation.

Amanda left the tiny satin-covered buttons unfastened so the camisole moved as she did, slipping and sliding back and forth lovingly as it clung to her cleavage, promising more than it revealed.

Kneeling on the plush vanity bench and knowing how provocative her saucy bottom looked resting on the heels of her soft white kid boots, she began applying her makeup with a light hand. Checking the shading of the pink and pale blue shadow she was applying to her eyelids had her rocking to and fro as she leaned in close, then pulled back to study the effect in the mirror.

The bed squeaked again.

Well, at least she knew she was keeping him awake, she thought with a secret smile. But he wasn't losing control, and it was beginning to annoy the hell out of her.

The style of clothing he'd picked out for her to wear seemed to call for an old-fashioned hairstyle, so she began repairing her topknot. Each time she reached up, her camisole would shift. Occasionally there would be a flash of her nipple, and then the silky material of the camisole would slide to quickly conceal what it had revealed.

Behind her, Kyle cleared his throat but said nothing.

She was so turned on she could barely breathe. How could he continue to just sit there and watch?

Why didn't he say something? *Do* something!

Never mind their differences—she wanted him.

Her eyes narrowed as she looked in the mirror and watched herself slowly fasten the tiny buttons of the frilly camisole, then tie the narrow slip of ribbon at the top into a sweet bow.

She didn't feel sweet. She didn't feel demure. She didn't feel like wearing all this white frilly stuff.

What she felt was wicked and sexy.

She felt like black lace and leather.

Frustrated, she picked up the silver-backed antique brush from her dressing table and smoothed an errant dark tendril back into place. Then, standing, she went to the bed and took the matching silk charmeuse tap pants with fluted edges from the same box that had contained the camisole.

Facing the mirror, she bent from the waist and stepped into the tap pants, then began pulling them up her long legs. Halfway up, her eyes lingered on the antique silver brush at eye level on her dressing table.

That's it, she decided. She'd reached her breaking point. Kyle was going to move, all right.

Abandoning the tap pants in a tangle at her knees, she picked up the hairbrush. For the first time, she looked directly at Kyle's reflection in the mirror above the dressing table, and their eyes locked. Holding his gaze, she lowered the brush and began a slow, rhythmic ritual, brushing the soft, downy fuzz between her legs.

He moved.

Bolting from the bed, Kyle reached her side in two long strides. His hand clamped on her wrist, stilling the brush.

"Think you're pretty cute, do you?" he asked, his voice all husky whisper. Before she could answer, he took the brush from her and pulled her over his knee as he dropped to the vanity bench.

"What do you think you're doing?" she demanded, squirming in his lap, letting out a small gasp as she felt the evidence of her successful seduction press against her soft belly.

"I'm giving you what you've been asking for," he answered, giving the brush a quick flick of his wrist to apply a few playful slaps to her inviting bare bottom.

"Now behave yourself and get dressed," he instructed, setting her back on her feet before he rose and headed for the stairs.

"Where are you going?" she asked, staring at his wide, retreating back in amazement.

He stopped in his tracks, but he didn't turn around to look at her.

"Downstairs. Come down when you're finished dressing."

"Downstairs?"

His words when he got them out were low and clipped. "I need a drink."

Without looking back, he headed down the stairs.

Amanda glared at the spot where he'd stood.

Turning, she stared at her reflection in the mirror, then picked up the hairbrush he'd set back on the dressing table and threw it against the wall in frustration. It landed with a thud, then skittered under the bed.

Her opinion of him hadn't changed. He was still the *most* aggravating, conceited, annoying, arrogant . . . handsome, sexy, exciting . . .

She finished dressing in a royal snit.

There had to be some way to get back at him for ignoring her attempt at seduction. Like most handsome men he was one of those dance-away lovers, flirting and teasing until you responded. Real sexuality in women scared them to death. She knew that. The men she'd dated back East had taught her.

As long as you said, "Oh sir, what are you doing, you naughty man?" and played the inferior innocent, they could function. It was when you demanded and gave equal time that they fled. Macho men couldn't handle women . . . only girls.

As she slipped into the white Victorian-style dress he'd picked out, Amanda's quick mind searched for a way to get her revenge on Kyle's abandoned seduction.

Her eyes lit up at a sudden idea the dress gave her as she tied the sash in a bow at her back. She looked in the mirror at her reflection one final time. The dress was exquisite.

It deserved to be seen at the finest restaurant in town. Finest equaled most expensive, she schemed...recalling that Kyle had said he'd take her someplace special when she was dressed.

Of course, they'd have to go to his place while he changed out of his cowboy duster, boots, frayed jeans and faded chambray shirt.

Turnabout. She could watch him dress. Yes, she was liking her idea better and better.

There was a smug smile on her face as she left her bedroom to join Kyle downstairs to put her plan for revenge into action. Before she was done with him, he was going to need a lot of drinks.

When she reached the top of the stairs, all the lights in the house went out at once, pitching it into sudden, complete darkness.

"Kyle...."

There was no answer.

10

AMANDA TOOK A TENTATIVE step down the stairs.

"Kyle. . . ." she whispered again into the darkness below.

There was no answer.

Her heart began to pound as she slid her hand along the smooth banister, edging her way down the stairs. When she was almost to the bottom, she heard a noise and froze.

As she stood immobile on the stairs, her eyes began adjusting to the darkness and she began surveying the room, identifying the dark shapes as furniture.

Suddenly a match flared.

She jumped and let out a startled gasp.

A man took shape in silhouette. After lighting a cheroot, he leaned to put the match to a candle, which shed a flickering glow to the room.

She could see now that the man leaning against her armoire was Kyle. Though his face was in shadow, she recognized the long cowboy duster.

He unfolded his arms and moved away from the armoire, adopting a threatening stance, his feet spread wide. His right hand moved to push the cowboy duster back from his right side.

Her eyes widened as the candlelight glinted off the silver buckle of a gun belt slung low across his lean hips.

The holster tied to his thigh with rawhide contained a pearl-handled revolver.

Drawing it, he leveled it on her like a gunfighter. His eyes glittered as he motioned for her to step forward.

Amanda did as he wanted, keeping her eyes on the revolver.

"Start taking it off, lady."

Her eyes wide, Amanda didn't move.

"Now."

She swallowed. Her hands reached behind her to untie the sash of the white Victorian dress, then moved to undo the row of tiny pearl buttons. She looked up at him when she'd finished unfastening the last one.

He motioned with the revolver for her to continue.

She stepped out of the dress, standing before him in frilly white undergarments and laced-up ankle boots.

His blue eyes flickered over her with interest.

"Go on."

Amanda's hand reached to untie the ribbon on her camisole, then moved to the satin-covered buttons. When all the little buttons were undone, the camisole parted and the candlelight flickered over her shadowed cleavage.

"Take it off."

Amanda hesitated and he cocked the revolver, motioning with his squared chin for her to do as he said.

The camisole slid to the floor.

His mouth slid into a tantalizing smile. "Pert little thing, aren't you?" he said as her nipples puckered impudently under his scrutiny.

Amanda's hands moved to cover them.

"Uh-uh."

She lowered her hands under his demanding stare.

"That's better. Now undo your hair."

Amanda reached to do his bidding, scattering hairpins to the floor around her. When her thick tresses fell to her shoulders, she didn't have to be told to shake it out.

Kyle stood studying her, the cloud of hair framing her beauty. She could have stepped right out of a history book—every cowboy's wet dream.

He uncocked the gun and laid it on the armoire.

"Come here."

Amanda crossed the distance between them with quick steps and threw her arms around him. Looking up into his laughing eyes, she said, "Think you're pretty cute, do you?"

He didn't bother to answer, but lifted her up into his arms and carried her upstairs to show her he was real cute, kissing her senseless along the way.

"You, sir, are no gentleman," Amanda sputtered when he tossed her unceremoniously in a heap in the middle of her brass bed. He put a match to another candle. "I know, ma'am. But then, when you conjured me up, you weren't exactly having thoughts about gentlemen, now, were you?" Kyle's grin was wicked as he pulled off his cowboy duster and tossed it over her vanity bench.

"Oh, dear. I suppose this means you're going to have your way with me," she said, pretending wide-eyed coyness as she sat in the middle of the bed, covering her bare breasts with her hands.

Kyle stopped what he was doing and looked at her. "My way, your way and every which way," he promised in a growl that sent delicious shivers down her spine.

"Oh, goody!"

Kyle's eyebrow arched. "'Oh, goody'?"

Amanda looked up at him, fluttering her eyelashes demurely. "Just one of my sweet little virginal expressions."

His hand stopped abruptly in the midst of unbuttoning his chambray shirt. "You're not . . ."

"That's right. I'm not," she said, watching his reaction.

He appeared to be real glad, scoring major points with her. Rising to her knees, she crawled over to the side of the bed where he was undressing. Her look was anything but demure as she trailed her tongue over the ridges of his hard, flat belly.

"Uh . . . Kyle?" she whispered up to him.

"Um . . . ?"

"When?"

"'When?'" he repeated on a groan as she detoured her tongue to his turgid nipple.

She looked up at him with a temptress's smile. "Uh-huh. When are you going to have your way with me?"

"If it's not soon," he said on an indrawn breath as she raked her teeth playfully over his nipple, "I'm afraid I'm going to die with my boots on."

Amanda's eyes slid down to the hard bulge behind the frayed fly of his jeans. "My, my. I thought you left your gun downstairs, Sundance."

"Us bad guys always have one on us," he said, giving up on unbuttoning the cuffs of his shirt and pulling them over his wrists. The buttons popped, and one of them flew against the brass headboard with a ping.

"Oh, you mean it's something like an itty-bitty derringer?" she squeaked, getting even with him for toying with her earlier.

Kyle cast her a maligning look as he unbuckled the empty gun belt and discarded it on the floor. "Why don't you see for yourself?" he dared.

Amanda's eyes grew wide, and she placed her hand flat against her chest. "Why, I couldn't do that, sir. It might . . . well, it might go off in my hand."

Kyle chuckled. "You're right. It might at that."

Reaching down with his hand to cup the soft swell of her breast, he captured her lips in an eating kiss, his tongue thrusting into the warm, moist sweetness of her mouth.

His breathing grew ragged and he pulled back, his hand slipping down to explore under the fluted edges of her tap pants. She emitted a strangled moan of pleasure when the heel of his palm ground into her pelvic bone.

"Do you think you could do me a favor?" he whispered hoarsely, his fingers teasing the throbbing dampness.

Amanda's head fell back, her eyes closed, and her body trembled with desire. "Anything, sir. Whatever you want. I'll stable your horse, sew on your buttons, kill the sheriff . . . anything. Just let me do it . . . umm . . . later."

"Uh-uh. I need you to do it now, Amanda."

"Now?"

"You don't want me to die with my boots on, do you?"

Amanda's eyes fluttered open. "Your boots?"

Kyle nodded. "I need your help getting them off."

"Oh."

She took a deep, calming breath and moved off the bed while Kyle sprawled back across it and closed his eyes. He was long, lean and flat, except for the straining protuberance at his crotch. Every inch of him was sexy and golden, even the hollows of his armpits.

Looking down at him, Amanda knew she was probably making a mistake, but like Scarlett, she'd worry about it tomorrow.

"My boots, ma'am," Kyle said, opening his eyes to see what the holdup was.

Amanda reached down, lifted up his boot by the heel and toe and tried pulling it toward her. It didn't come off. She took a deep breath and tried again. Nothing.

Kyle, watching her, shook his head disparagingly. "Lady, don't you know nothing about cowboys? You're doing it all wrong."

"I am?"

"Uh-huh. See, you've got to swing your leg over my boot like it's a horse.... That's it. And then... umph... pull."

He teased her by wiggling his ankle, wedging his boot up against her femininity. "Kyle!"

"Yes, ma'am."

"Behave."

"Yes, ma'am," he answered, sliding his boot back and forth, ignoring her instructions with a naughty chuckle.

Without any help from him, she managed to get both his boots off and herself as frustrated as sin.

Turning on him, she demanded, "What do you call that?"

"A lesson," he said with a wink, pulling her down against him, where he began kissing her throat with hot, openmouthed kisses. "Now you know why ladies love cowboys and cowboys never, ever die with their boots on."

"You're incorrigible." She laughed lustily.

"Yes, ma'am."

He pulled her over him on her knees, her thighs straddling his chest. Proving just how incorrigible he was, he slid his hands up the backs of her stockings, grazing the bare thighs above and then on up beneath the fluted edges of her tap pants. Squeezing her sleek buttocks rhythmically, he brought the juncture of her thighs to his mouth, sucking at her through the silky material, his teeth nipping maddeningly.

Removing one hand to pull pillows beneath his head, he propped himself up so he could give her uptilted breasts the same lavish attention.

His tongue flicked back and forth across their peaks until they were hard and puckered. Then, opening his mouth wide, he began paying homage to their thrusting invitation as he laved and sucked until he heard Amanda's breathy little moans.

His lips slid lower, and he rained darting, then lingering kisses over her lower abdomen, teasing her, his hands still kneading and squeezing her bottom rhythmically.

His nose edged beneath the fluted tap pants provocatively. Her moisture and the dampness of his mouth soon mingled, drenching the scrap of silk and filling the air with the heady scent of sex. Within moments, his ears rang with her joyful whimpers of pleasure as she convulsed against his cheek, his hands working their magic until she quieted.

Pulling her down against him, he folded her in his arms, covering her with gentle kisses and sweet love words. When her breathing returned to normal, he rolled over and got up from the bed. Unsnapping his jeans, he dug something from his pocket before he shucked the jeans from his body and kicked them aside impatiently.

A moment later he rejoined her on the bed, pulling her close.

"Touch me," he whispered hoarsely, pulling her hand down to his hardness.

"So. You are a gentleman, after all," she said, feeling the protection he'd used.

She felt his eyelashes flutter closed against her cheeks as a shudder of pleasure rippled over him at her intimate caress.

"Amanda...." He sighed worshipfully.

She opened her mouth to his, and they supped hungrily, their tongues exploring and mating.

"I can't wait any longer," he groaned, his breath ragged and uneven.

Levering himself above her, he tugged the silky tap pants to her knees. "Now let's go 'someplace special' together."

"Yes," Amanda cried, arching up to meet his thrust as he entered her velvet-soft slickness.

He went up on his knees as he surged again, pulling her with him. Her back arched away from him as she braced herself on her palms. Shivers of pleasure raced along her nerve endings when he lowered his lips to her upturned breasts and sucked them, his hands on her hips continuing to pull her to his hard, deep thrusts.

One hand surged into her dark tresses, pulling her torso up against his. His golden body hair swirling over his wide, sculptured chest abraded her sensitive breasts. When he withdrew slowly, almost completely, then entered her with a quick succession of thrusts, she bit into his shoulder and screamed with the shock of pure pleasure that rocked her.

Kyle lost any vestige of control at her cry of pleasure. He threw back his head, his eyes closed, his mouth open, and ground his groin against her as he throbbed to climax.

They clung to each other, damp and slick . . . breathless.

When the final tremors of passion ebbed, they collapsed in an embrace of limp satisfaction.

Beside her, Amanda felt Kyle's lips move against her ear. "I think you just ruined fantasy for me, lady."

"Does that mean you had a *real good* time?" Amanda purred.

"Umm. . . ." he murmured, nuzzling her ear. "I should have realized it was really my job and not my sexy body you were after. Much more of that and Noah would find himself notifying my next of kin."

"You mean that's all? We're done?" Amanda teased, leaning up on her elbow and playfully trailing her fingertips across his washboard belly.

"*I* am . . . but you go right ahead. Don't mind me." Punching up his pillow, he looked over at her with a Cheshire cat smile and said, "I'll watch."

Amanda kicked off her tap pants, which had ended up tangled at her ankles, and flipped over onto her stomach. "Not without the price of admission, you won't."

"'Price of admission'?"

"Uh-huh."

"I'm afraid to ask," he said, resting his hands behind his head.

"'Admission' is the operative word," she explained. "You mean I have to . . . ah . . . tell you something?"

"*Admit* to something," she clarified.

"Like what?"

"It can be anything. Deep, dark sexual secrets are good."

"Deep, dark . . ." His eyes widened. "Amanda!"

"I'm waiting. . . ."

"But I don't have any. . . Wait a minute, there was the time with the two airline stewardesses in the rest room of the plane. . . ."

"*Two* stewardesses?"

"Nah, come to think, that was my evil twin."

"What about your evil twin?" she asked, twirling a strand of his blond hair between her fingers.

"I can't tell. He's real shy and made me promise not to tell anyone about him."

"You're sure he exists?"

"He's been around as long as I can remember."

"I see."

Kyle turned and scooped her up.

"What are you doing?"

"I decided I don't want to watch, after all," he answered, whispering a very naughty suggestion into her ear.

AMANDA LAY PROPPED UP on her elbow, watching Kyle sleep. He looked as though he belonged there beside her on her bed. Even though he was asleep, his presence in the carriage house chased the loneliness from the rooms. If only he was in love with her.

The morning sunlight streaming in through the plantation shutters cast shafts of light, patterning him in a soft, golden glow. In sleep, he was beautifully innocent. His blond hair was mussed as if he'd raked his hands through it repeatedly. His sweeping lashes cast faint shadows on his pronounced cheekbones. A faint stubble showed on his angular jaw.

Her eyes lowered to his chest. She couldn't help herself. She had to touch him. Touch the golden blond hair matted there.... She laid her hand on his chest tentatively. When he didn't move, she slid her hand across him in a loving caress.

Kyle's laugh was rich and lusty as he caught her hand in his strong grip.

"Am I dead?" he asked, opening one eye and looking over at her.

" 'Dead'?"

"I seem to remember being in heaven last night," he said, bringing her hand to his lips for a nibbling kiss.

The sleepy sensuality in his eyes made her stomach somersault as he considered her.

She would have enjoyed the compliment and the scrutiny if he wasn't looking so pleased with himself.

"That's funny. I seem to remember being with a devil, myself," she retorted.

His rich, lusty chuckle sounded again as he shook his head at her. "Amanda, love, what am I going to do with you?"

"Well, sir, if you're truly open to suggestions, I do have an idea or two. . . ."

Much later that morning, while Kyle was showering, Amanda sat before her dressing table brushing her hair while trying to decide how to broach the subject of her job offer to Kyle.

The shower stopped and Kyle joined her, blithely toweling off as he searched for his clothes. She knew if she didn't plunge right in and tell him, she would become addle-brained from looking at an unselfconsciously naked man dressing in her bedroom.

"Uh . . . Kyle?"

He looked up from zipping his jeans.

"We need to talk. . . ." she began.

"I know. I—"

"It's about our working together," she said, interrupting before she lost her nerve. "I think it's only fair that I tell you I've had another job offer. It's a great opportunity for me."

"Who with?" he asked, looking away.

Amanda named the New York television syndicate.

"I see." Kyle got very quiet as he snapped his jeans. "You're going to take it, then?" he asked finally, after pulling on his boots. He still hadn't looked at her.

"I haven't made up my mind yet. I've still got a week left to decide."

He didn't comment. Finding his faded blue chambray shirt, he put it on, rolling up the sleeves when he encountered the missing buttons he'd popped off the cuffs in the rush of passion.

"What do you think I should do?" she asked into the quiet, holding her breath, hoping for the words she wanted so desperately to hear.

He looked over at her at last. "I think you should take it," he advised, his clear blue eyes void of emotion.

She let out her breath on a long, silent sigh. He hadn't asked her to stay, as she'd hoped. Not that she would give up a job opportunity for a man, but it would have meant everything for him to have made it a consideration . . . for him to have given some indication that he cared.

Walking toward her, he stopped and picked up his cowboy duster from the floor beside her and threw it over his shoulder.

His smile, when he bent to brush a kiss on her nose, was weak. "I've got to go."

Did he care? she dared to hope again.

"Really, you think I should take the job?" she asked, giving him another chance to voice his feelings.

He nodded, his feelings remaining carefully hidden. "Yeah, like you said, it's a terrific opportunity."

"What about—" she couldn't stop herself from asking.

"Us?" He supplied the obvious, finishing her thought.

She nodded.

His smile was rueful.

"Maybe it was just a great fantasy, you know?" he said, turning to go.

KYLE SPENT THE REST of the week pondering how very good Amanda had felt in his arms. How very right.

Needs, long repressed, had surfaced.

He had closed himself off long ago, he now realized, living only in the dark rooms of his fantasies. Amanda had somehow gotten inside those dark rooms.

Her news of a job opportunity in New York had been like a swift kick in the gut. He'd been about to allow himself to care for her, when she as much as told him she was leaving.

He didn't want her to give up the opportunity, but he didn't want her to go, either. If she stayed, it had to be her choice, but he didn't hold out much hope that she would.

He gazed down at the envelope in his hand. When he had seen her purse on the desk in her living room, he hadn't been able to resist slipping the fantasy she'd written for Oscar night from it on his way out.

Resting his hip on the edge of his desk, he picked up a letter opener and slit open the pale pink envelope to read the single sheet of matching stationery inside.

There was only one sentence.

Kyle,
I want to make love with you and your best friend together.

Kyle laughed out loud, his gloomy mood dispelled. Why, that little minx!

She hadn't played fair at all. He knew without a doubt that she thought she'd come up with a fantasy he wouldn't do, just in case she won.

She'd thought wrong, Kyle decided, a smile tugging the corners of his lips.

She may not stay, but when she got to New York, he wasn't going to be so easy to forget.... Amanda was about to find out how perverse he could be. She was about to meet his evil twin.

11

SATURDAY AFTERNOON Amanda sat at her desk working on a review of the movie she'd just seen, but her
mind kept straying. She hadn't been alone with Kyle
since the morning after their night together. She was
sure he was purposely avoiding her, glad even of her
news of a job offer in New York. He'd gotten what he
wanted. Heaven forbid he get tangled up in something
he didn't want, like a commitment.

She'd thought she would be able to chalk up their
night together as a night of pleasure, a fantasy shared,
nothing more. But it had been more to her; they'd made
love, not just had sex.

When her doorbell rang, it distracted her from her
all too frequent thoughts of Kyle and their magic night
together.

"Amanda...."

It was him!

"Go away," she called crossly, wanting him to do no
such thing.

"Aw, come on Amanda, sweet. Let us in."

"Go away."

"You'd best do as he says, little lady," an unfamiliar
voice said in a Texas drawl.

Curiosity won out over petulance, and she went to
open the door.

Kyle stood before her when she swung open the door. He was alone.

"Didn't I hear someone else out here with you?" she asked in a puzzled voice, standing on tiptoe and trying in vain to look over his wide shoulder.

"That was my evil twin I'm always telling you about," Kyle explained. "I thought it was time you met him."

"Your evil twin," Amanda repeated, looking doubtful. "So where is he?"

"Oh, he'll be right back. I had to send him to pick up something I forgot."

"Something you forgot...." Amanda said, waiting for his nose to grow.

Kyle grinned. "Yeah, I didn't remember till we got here that you were all out of whipped cream."

He was kidding her. Yes, that was it. She looked around him to the street to check on his Mustang, just in case. It wasn't there.

Kyle took advantage of her distraction to slip inside the carriage house. "When he gets back, it'll be your turn," he called back over his shoulder nonchalantly.

"What *are* you talking about?" she demanded, following him inside.

Kyle's eyes grew devilish as he slipped the pink envelope containing Amanda's Oscar-night fantasy from the pocket of his bomber jacket.

"*This* is what I'm talking about," he answered, waggling the slender pink envelope between his long fingers.

"Where did you get that?" she cried, trying to snatch it from him.

"I stole it from your purse," he said without a shred of remorse.

She looked up at him when she saw the ragged edges of the envelope, the broken seal signaling it had been opened.

"Yes, I read it," he said in answer to her silent accusation. "We both did."

"'Both'?"

Kyle shrugged. "Well, he's my evil twin, but he's also my best friend, and I needed to make sure he'd go along with your . . . ahem . . . unusual request."

"But I didn't mean. . ." Amanda objected as she stared at him in openmouthed amazement.

"It's okay, really," Kyle assured her. "He won't tell. He's *never* told on me."

"Kyle, we can't—"

"Why, sure we can. Actually, he thinks it's a really hot idea. Course, he is my *evil* twin—you know, the two stewardesses and all. . . ."

"*Kyle!*"

"Chicken," Kyle taunted with a heavy-lidded stare.

"I'm not. It's just—"

"Yes . . . ?" Kyle coaxed, his features impassive as he considered her. "What you're trying to tell me is that *this*—" he waved the pink envelope in his hand "—is not a fantasy of yours, that you didn't play fair. Is that what you're trying to tell me, Amanda?"

She sighed. She knew a double bind when she walked into one. "Okay, I admit it's a fantasy of mine, but it's not something I could ever—"

"You could with me."

She could? He wouldn't. That was the reason she'd made it her choice on Oscar night. He was only bluffing. There was no evil twin. There was only him taunting her.

She smiled.

Okay, she'd take him up on his dare, she decided, ignoring the little voice in her head reminding her of her promise to never, ever take another dare.

"There's just one thing," Kyle said, pulling a silk scarf from the pocket of his bomber jacket. "Remember what I said about my evil twin being shy? Well, he won't do this unless you're blindfolded."

So that was how he planned to pull it off. He was going to play out the bluff. He wasn't going to give in.

Well, she wasn't going to give in, either. "Okay," she agreed, sitting down on the love seat. "You and your evil twin . . .

What was his name?"

"Lyle," Kyle supplied.

"*Lyle?*"

"Momma is English," Kyle said with a shrug, as if that explained it.

Amanda tried to keep from giggling. *Lyle!* Mercy.

"Well," she said when she had her merriment under control, "Lyle and you had better be great together, because this is one of my favorite fantasies, and if you ruin it for me, I'll never, ever forgive you."

"Not to worry, Amanda," Kyle promised with a wicked wink as he began folding the silk scarf into a bandanna. "Momma always did say what one of us didn't think of, the other one would."

Kyle tied the bandanna around her head securely. "Did you hear that? It must be Lyle at the door now," he said, answering his own question while Amanda tried not to laugh.

Kyle really was playing it for all it was worth, and she wondered how far she would let him go before she lost her nerve. Why had she ever told him about her weakness when it came to dares? That was like giving a rat the key to a warehouse full of cheese. She must be an idiot.

Kyle moved away from her, and she heard the front door open and close.

"Say hello, Lyle," Amanda heard Kyle say.

"Well, hello, pretty lady. Hey, are you sure you want to do this? My brother here, why, he can be a bit of a rascal sometimes. Did he ever tell you about the two stewardesses... No, wait. I think that was me." He chuckled. "Sometimes I forget which one of us did what."

"She's sure," Kyle said for her.

The currents in the room crackled with electricity as she felt her blouse being pushed down her arms and warm lips caressing a pathway along her throat.

And then the caressing stopped suddenly.

"Well, I'll be tongue-tied, if she ain't the angel you said she was. Her skin's as white and soft as a perfect pearl," Kyle observed in a hushed drawl as Amanda felt her blouse slip all the way off.

In moments she was sitting before them—him—naked, her body responding to the stimuli of touch and whispered sexy encouragements. She sat very straight on the love seat, her legs a little apart, because in her excitement she could not keep them together. Her skin was on fire as she imagined eyes lingering *everywhere*.

"Lyle's into feet, Amanda. You don't mind, do you?" Kyle asked as she felt hands smoothing over the arch of her foot and massaging the pad below her toes . . . familiarly.

She gasped when a wet tongue began to lick between her toes and then slipped them between lips that sucked provocatively.

"Umm, little lady, why I swear, y'all have got the most precious toes I've ever laid eyes on."

Amanda pulled her foot away, beginning to get very nervous.

At that moment she was eased to her feet, her face held in the V of a thumb and forefinger. His tongue thrust between her lips, burying itself in her moist sweetness, while he brought her naked body into full contact with his.

He was still fully dressed. She could feel the soft T-shirt against her bare breasts, the texture of his jeans sliding against her thighs, the erotic stab of his belt buckle. And she was rubbing up against him shamelessly. It was Kyle. She knew the size and shape of him intimately. But then if Lyle was his *twin* . . .

Before she could continue with that thought, his hands clutched her shoulders, then slid slowly down her back, pressing her closer until he cupped her buttocks; his long, supple fingers kneading, squeezing, separating and then lifting. He groaned an exquisite male shudder of need when he ground against her. And then he took a deep, satisfying breath and went very still before moving away from her.

She gave a little cry of desertion when she heard the front door open and close.

"Kyle. . . ."

"He had to leave, darlin'. Something about a movie he had to review. But I've got the rest of the afternoon free."

Amanda's eyes flew open as the blindfold was torn from her. She was almost surprised to see Kyle standing there before her.

"I couldn't stay away any longer," Kyle said. "I tried, but Lyle wouldn't let me. He's always talking me into doing these dangerous things. He told me if I let a woman like you go because I was afraid, he would never speak to me again."

Amanda smiled. "Let me give you a kiss for Lyle," she said, wrapping her arms around his neck as he carried her upstairs.

When they reached the top of the stairs, she giggled.

"What?" he demanded.

"Once again, I'm naked and you're not."

"There's a reason for that."

"Don't try telling me you're bashful."

"Only with my clothes on. You see, when I take off all my clothes, I turn into an animal." His smile was wicked and as cocky as hell.

"Kyle . . ." Her tongue was exploring his ear.

"Hmm?" he asked, carrying her to the bed.

"Shut up and . . ." She was now biting his neck.

"And?" The word was slurred as his mouth closed over her breast.

"Take off—oh!—um . . . all your clothes."

He looked up from what he was doing, pleased with himself. "If you insist, ma'am." He deposited her gently on the bed.

"And Kyle . . ." she said, insisting with her hands as she pulled down his jeans.

"Hmm?" He kicked free of his jeans before looking up at her.

She dipped her hands inside his briefs. "Don't call me ma'am."

"Why? Aren't you a lady?" he dared, discarding his briefs and slapping playfully at her roaming hands.

She covered his cocky smile with her mouth and showed him she'd left her manners at the door.

EACH SUCCEEDING DAY brought with it a rush of happiness and wonder as they explored their tender new relationship. But time was running out for her to give New York a decision about the job offer.

She was certain Noah planned to renew her contract after the success of the theme shows and the surge in *Theater Talk*'s ratings. And she had grown fond of Noah. It would be difficult to leave so soon after he'd given her her big break.

It would be even more difficult to leave Kyle. She'd tried to bring up the subject of the job offer to him several times, but he'd insisted it was her decision and refused to discuss it. What would her taking the job do to their budding relationship? she pondered. Would he be able to handle her being more successful than he?

He would have to. She didn't intend to follow in her mother's footsteps—living her life around a man, subject to only his wants and needs.

But she didn't want to spend her life without Kyle, either.

She was no closer to a decision when she left to get the makings for the dinner she'd invited Kyle to. Inside her car she found an envelope lying on the seat with her name scrawled across it in Kyle's bold handwriting.

Amanda, precious,

It's a plum shame my twin brother, Kyle, made me leave the other day just when things were getting real interesting. Darlin', if you ask me, it was downright criminal on his part.

Criminal. . . . That conjures up some images, don't it? Let me show you how bad I can really be. . . .

We're aboard the Great Southern Chesapeake train. A porter in a white jacket brings your coffee. As he pours, you look up to observe that the dark, wood-paneled dining car is empty, save the two men sitting at a table across the aisle.

We are sitting side by side at our dining table, which might be unusual for two men, except for the obvious handcuffs explaining that one of us is a prisoner. . . a criminal. It's the one watching you.

You give a little gasp when you catch my eye. You've felt me looking at you all along, haven't you?

I don't look away, do I?

Neither can you. Something primitive is happening inside you, isn't it? Your heart races as little shivers of excitement unnerve you.

You look away finally, finish your coffee quickly and flee to the safety of your compartment. But my broad, villainous mustache and clear blue "don't give a damn" eyes continue to haunt you.

There's a knock on the door of the compartment, and you give a start of surprise to discover by sheer coincidence that we are sharing the same compartment. We both join you.

The man holding me prisoner tips his hat in deference to you. I give you none; my expression is sexy...sullen. Suddenly you're certain I'm a terrific kisser, and you blush, afraid I know somehow about the sexual stirrings I've elicited against your will.

We take our place opposite you on the deeply cushioned seat and sit facing you. The compartment is dark except for the lamp you've been reading by. Before long, the man I'm handcuffed to begins to snore softly.

You look over at me cautiously, at the man you are sure will break any rule. My wicked smile of acknowledgment and frank appraisal is aggressively male. You close your eyes against it's sensual suggestion

While you're thrilled by the fact that I'm dangerous and unpredictable, you feel safe. You know I'm unable to make a move without alerting the man holding me prisoner. So you allow yourself your own provocative thoughts....

In your fantasy, you feel the cushioned seat beside you give as I sit down to join you. Keeping your eyes closed, you pretend not to notice, but your silky eyelashes flutter briefly when I run my leather-gloved thumb along your jaw.

My lips soon follow, finding your own to acknowledge with experienced certainty that I am indeed a terrific kisser. . . .

Your hands seem to have a mind of their own as they begin their exploration. Quickly, you undo the buttons of my shirt, opening it wide so you can access my sleek, muscled chest. Your fingertip flicks my nipple teasingly and then travels downward, caressing the hard indentations of my belly.

There is a quick intake of breath when you discover the scar left by a knife. You lower your head, your lips bestowing a kiss to make it all better. Alas, the heel of your hand discovers your kiss has made it all worse as the evidence of my arousal strains behind my belt buckle.

You start to pull away, but my strong grip holds you as my other hand unfastens my belt and tucks your hand inside my pants to feel my warm, hard, satiny desire.

The train suddenly begins to slow, and the sound of metal grinding on metal signals we are making a stop. I push your hand away and get up quickly. When the train comes to a full stop, you open your eyes and look over. The man beside me is still asleep.

My eyes are on you . . . all over you. You blush. Surely, you think, the prisoner can't know what you've been daydreaming.

Daydreaming? It had seemed so real. . . . But, no, you are being foolish, believing the knowledge I pretend with my knowing eyes.

Blue eyes that suddenly wink as I slip my hand from the handcuff and rub my wrist before slipping it back.

No!

Yes!

You know somewhere along the line I'm going to escape. And you also know I'm not going to forget you. I'll be back to finish what we started. . . .

Lyle

Amanda refolded the fantasy letter and took a deep, shaky breath. Kyle didn't play fair, not fair at all. How was she going to leave him and go to New York?

By the time she arrived at the market, she'd managed to remember what she was shopping for and headed for the produce aisle, selecting crisp, fresh makings for a salad. But when she got to the bakery section to pick up French bread and dessert, she saw Kyle peering into the glass bakery case, the backs of his hands resting casually on his narrow hips. She hung back, watching him.

Her lazy green eyes slid covetously down his body, enjoying the taut, lean muscles. A slim, expensive belt at his narrow waist anchored a pair of snug jeans. Faded and threadbare, the jeans looked more in danger of disintegrating than of falling from his lean hips.

She continued to savor him, silently approving his good taste in cookies as he indicated her favorite chocolate chips to the bakery clerk. When the clerk had mounded the last of the chocolate chip cookies on the scale, Amanda edged forward.

"A gentleman wouldn't take the very last cookie," she whispered, her voice playful and inviting.

He turned. His eyes registered his pleasure at seeing her, and the beginnings of a smile emboldened her to carry on.

"It's ridiculous, I know, but I can't seem to go to bed without them." She smiled sheepishly. "I'm a bit obsessive about having my warm chocolate chip cookies every night."

The promised smile dawned. " 'Warm'?"

"Uh-huh. I pop them into the microwave, and they get all warm and gooey. I . . . ah . . . could show you, if you're gentleman enough to share the last of the cookies."

Kyle crooked his elbow around her neck and pulled her toward him affectionately. "You just wait till I get you home."

The bakery clerk had piled the cookies on a Styrofoam tray, wrapped them in cellophane and was sliding them toward him. Kyle picked them up and released her.

"I'll meet you at your place," he said, heading for the checkout counter with the cookies and a bottle of wine.

Amanda watched his bare feet nestled in a pair of lived-in topsiders as he walked away. Her eyes traveled back up to his jeans and lingered. He had a wonderful walk. He was endearingly pigeon-toed, and it did something incredibly sexy to his gait.

With a sigh, she gathered her confused thoughts and stepped up to the counter to place her order for a loaf of French bread. The young girl behind the counter slid the crusty, still-warm bread into a paper sleeve. As Amanda took it from the clerk, she inhaled it's yeasty warmth and began to feel a little better. Few things in life were more comforting than the aroma of fresh baked bread. She added it to her cart, then started for the jam of shoppers at the checkout lanes.

There were only two shoppers ahead of Kyle in the quick line. She got in line behind him. Her vantage point afforded her an intimate view of the man. She averted her eyes to his hands, cradling his tray of chocolate chip cookies possessively. She wished his hands were holding her with the same degree of possession. She closed her eyes and could almost feel his long, sensitive fingers touching her skin, smell the clean, just-showered scent of him, even feel his warm breath on her cheek—

"Timmy! Look out!"

Amanda turned at the woman's shriek. But not in time. A little towheaded boy rammed her cart, knocking her off balance. Clutching wildly for anything to break her fall, she gripped something at last. A hard thigh. And then she heard a loud rip as her fingers caught on a hole in the soft, frayed denim.

There was a flash of tanned, hairy thigh before her eyes as she slid slowly toward the floor, hoping against hope a large hole would be waiting to swallow her up. Alas, before she reached the floor, strong hands were rescuing her, pulling her up against his chest. She looked down in an attempt to avoid his incredulous blue eyes, only to see the smashed tray of what were now chocolate chip crumbs by her feet. There was a lull, quiet and pregnant as she glanced up at him.

"Are you all right?" he asked, coughing to smother the laughter that was threatening to erupt at the outraged mortification reflected in her sweet green eyes.

And then it dawned on her that he wasn't the least bit embarrassed. Not the least bit. Why, he looked . . . he looked amused.

She realized then that she was clinging to him like a sacrificial virgin confronted with the mouth of a volcano.

"Yes . . . yes. I'm fine," she answered in a hoarse whisper, straightening in his arms. "But I'm afraid I've ripped your thigh . . . er . . . pants," she corrected hastily, cursing the imagery in her mind. "And I've crumbled your cookies," she blurted without thinking.

That did it. He doubled over with boisterous laughter.

When he got his merriment under control, he bent and whispered, "That seals it. Guess you're going to have to marry me now."

But there was no more talk of marriage during the evening that ensued. At the carriage house, Amanda loaned Kyle one of her oversize robes and had begun mending his ancient jeans as best she could when he returned from the bathroom dressed in the navy terry cloth. The living room suddenly grew smaller. She yelped when she stuck herself with the needle while staring absently at his hands knotting the robe's sash.

Quickly finishing the mending, she shoved the jeans at Kyle and went to make the salad for dinner.

He didn't change for dinner, but remained in the robe. Any other man would have changed into his jeans immediately, but Kyle seemed comfortable dressed in next to nothing.

After dinner he helped her with the dishes, and then they sat down to watch a movie she had on tape.

When the opening credits for the televised version of *The Long Hot Summer* appeared, Kyle voiced his approval. "Good choice. The actress who played Varner's son's wife was terrific in this."

"I beg your pardon?"

"You don't agree?"

"Are you kidding? The male lead stole that movie away from everyone."

"Admit it, Amanda, you went for his sex appeal."

"Exactly," Amanda agreed with a wicked smile.

"Why, Amanda Butterworth, I'm surprised at you! I'da thought you were too smart to be tempted by a bare-chested man in a pair of unsnapped jeans on a veranda," he teased, referring to the fantasy he'd written her, as well as the movie.

Amanda laughed. "Honey, ain't no woman alive that smart," she drawled in her best southern belle accent.

She was joking, but she was also wondering if it was true. Would she be copping out if she didn't take the job the New York television syndicate had offered her?

Was she kidding herself, believing the reasons she kept making up to stay and pursue their relationship over taking the promotion? She had always promised herself an independent life. Promised herself she wouldn't take a back seat to a man.

But any relationship called for some compromises, didn't it? It was foolish to draw hard-and-fast lines in a society where rapid change was the only constant. If she made a decision not to take the job at this time in her life, it didn't mean she wouldn't take another offer. If she believed in herself, then she had to believe there would be another offer.

She had her answer. She would pass up the promotion this time, allowing her personal life precedence now. Her relationship with Kyle was important and too new to survive the separation. And she still had room to learn and grow in her current position.

Having made the decision, she couldn't wait until the movie was over to tell Kyle, so she began tickling him to distract him.

"Amanda! Come on, quit. I can't see the movie." He laughed as she ran her fingertips over the soles of his feet, knowing how ticklish his feet were.

She didn't quit while she was ahead.

The next thing she knew, Kyle had her pinned to the floor, a devilish gleam flickering in his eyes.

"So you want to play games with me, do you?" he teased, clamping her hands over her head with one hand while he wriggled the fingers of his free hand teasingly.

"No, don't," she pleaded unsuccessfully as Kyle began tickling her ribs.

Alternately squirming and giggling, she begged him to stop.

Pausing in his torment, he asked, "If I stop tickling, what will you promise me?"

"That I won't take the job offer," she blurted.

"What?" Kyle asked, taken completely by surprise.

"If you promise to stop tickling me, I won't take the job offer Westec made me," she answered.

"You're kidding."

She shook her head.

"Really?"

She nodded.

"When did you decide?" he asked, knowing tickling had nothing to do with her decision.

"A little while ago," she answered, taking his offered hand.

He helped her up from the floor and continued to worry her decision to turn down the job in New York.

"So how come you decided not to take Westec's offer?" he asked.

"I don't know," she answered. "Maybe because I'd miss your handsome face."

"Yeah, right, and there really is a Santa Claus. Tell me the real reason."

She shrugged. It was the real reason, or at least part of it. "I'd feel bad about leaving Noah so soon," she said finally.

KYLE HAD APPEARED pleased with her decision, but no further discussion ensued, as the following week was hectic. She and Kyle had to tape both a *Theater Talk* and a theme show. Unable to reach an agreement on foreign films or horror flicks, they'd compromised with comedies.

The week was filled with everything from amused smiles to raucous laughter as they previewed films for the theme show, attended a rock concert KCNX had sponsored and made fierce and tender love.

That Friday night after the tapings, Kyle had shown up on her doorstep with a wide smile and a duffel bag full of clean shirts, reminding her of her on-air promise to iron his shirts for a week.

Then he'd told her he thought it would be best if they spent the weekend apart, as he had something personal he needed to think about.

Amanda worried that she had misjudged Kyle's response to her not taking the job offer. Perhaps he'd only wanted a temporary fling, and now he was beginning to feel hemmed in. Was he spending the weekend trying to figure a way to break off their relationship?

12

SATURDAY MORNING DAWNED glorious with the promise of a warm spring day. Amanda threw open all the windows and set up her ironing board before the television so she could watch MTV as she ironed the shirts Kyle had dropped off. She'd do it this once to honor her words, she'd decided, but if they were married, he'd be taking them to the cleaner's, just as she did with her own.

She had to admit that it wasn't so bad doing his shirts. Each one she ironed reminded her of Kyle and the special times they'd spent together. As she hung up the last shirt, she brought it to her cheek. One night apart and already she missed him.

After she put away the iron and ironing board and hung his shirts in the entry closet for him to pick up, she turned off the television and sat down to read the morning newspaper with a cold glass of milk and a chocolate chip cookie warm from the microwave.

After skimming the first page, Amanda turned to the entertainment section to check on the new movie releases in theaters for the upcoming week. Picking up a pencil and pad, she made a note of the times of the movies she and Kyle would be reviewing for *Theater Talk*.

As she was refolding the entertainment section, her eye was caught by a small publicity photo of Kyle in the "About Town" gossip column. She made a mental note to have Toby send the newspaper one of the new publicity photos of her and Kyle together as she began to scan the column to see what the columnist was saying about *Theater Talk*.

As she read the piece, she nearly choked on her milk. She couldn't believe her eyes and began rereading it.

The latest scuttlebutt about KCNX's hot movie-review show, *Theater Talk*, is that one of it's co-hosts, Kyle Fox, is in the Big Apple this weekend being wooed by the Westec Syndicate. Wonder what his cohost, Amanda Butterworth, will have to say about that? Our bet is plenty.

Amanda threw down the newspaper as if it had suddenly caught fire in her hands.

Springing up from the love seat, she marched determinedly to the entry closet and yanked open the door. With great control, she removed every one of Kyle's carefully ironed shirts from its hanger, wadding each into a crumpled ball before throwing it to the floor. She slammed her closet door shut and jumped up and down on the pile of shirts in a fury. Then she shoved the lot into his duffel bag and threw it next to the front door.

She unclasped the diamond chip ankle bracelet Kyle had sweet-talked her into keeping, realizing now that it was the only kind of diamond he'd ever intended giving her. She had only been a pleasant and handy diversion. Wiping the tears from her damp cheeks, she reopened the duffel bag and tossed the glittering anklet inside. Stupid, stupid, stupid. She'd been a little fool.

Her hands were shaking as she dialed KCNX, using the number for Noah's private line.

Toby came on the line on the third ring.

"Is Noah in?" she asked, just managing to keep a sob from her voice.

"Yeah, he's around here someplace, Amanda. I'll tell him it's you on the line."

"No . . . uh, Toby? Just tell him I'm coming in to see him, okay?"

"Sure thing, Amanda," he answered, then heard the click as she hung up.

He hadn't had to ask any questions. He, too, had seen the morning newspaper. It was spread open on Noah's desk.

"HE'S GOING TO TAKE IT, isn't he?" Amanda said with resignation when she faced Noah across his desk a half hour later.

"I wouldn't be surprised," Noah answered, lifting the dish of candy mints in offering.

Amanda shook her head.

"Aren't you angry with him?" she cried as Noah slipped one of the mints into his mouth.

"Why?" Noah asked, leaning back in his chair.

"Why? Well, because he'd be leaving us—you—in the lurch. Doesn't he have a contract or something he has to honor—or doesn't he honor those, either?" she muttered, pacing back and forth nervously.

Noah smoothed his hand over his bald head, hating to see Amanda so distressed.

"Actually, he's been working without a contract for the past three months."

"What?"

Noah shrugged. "He's been restless lately and didn't want to make any long-term commitments. Since the ratings were falling on *Theater Talk*, I let it ride."

Noah's mention of Kyle's reluctance with long-term commitments made her quiet. She went over to look out the window at Noah's beloved view of the river.

Suddenly she turned and strode back to his desk. "What about now that the ratings have picked up?" she asked.

"Sure, I'd like to keep him," Noah agreed. "But when Kyle came to me and told me about Westec's offer, I told him to go for it, if that's what he wanted. I care about the boy, and there's no way I can match what they're offering, you know that."

"You knew about Westec's offer to Kyle and you didn't tell me?" she demanded, spreading her palms flat on Noah's desk and leaning forward in dismay.

"Did *you* tell me about your offer from Westec?" Noah countered quietly.

"You knew?"

Noah leaned forward in his chair and smiled. "There isn't much that goes on in the industry that's secret when you've been around as long as I have. You get to know a lot of people, have a lot of sources."

Amanda dropped into a nearby chair. "I would have told you, you know, if I had decided to take the job. In fact, you were part of the consideration, part of why I didn't take their offer," she added hastily, trying to make amends.

Noah rose from his desk and walked over to the window. Looking out, he said, "If you had come to me as Kyle did, I would have told you what I told him. I'm leaving KCNX in June."

"You're quitting?" Amanda exclaimed in surprise.

"I'm taking a year off," Noah said, turning with a smile. "It was my wife's idea. She knows how much I love the river, and she's talked me into buying a yacht. We're going to take off and cruise the waterways for a year. She thinks it's time I stopped to smell the roses, so to speak." He shook his head. "I don't know how I got so lucky to find a woman like her," he said with a dazed smile. The smile of a man deeply in love.

"But Noah, that's wonderful!" Amanda cried, thinking it would be time well spent getting rid of his ulcer and restoring his health.

Noah nodded and returned to his desk. "Why didn't you take the offer from Westec?"

"It came at the wrong time in my life." She shrugged. "Or so I thought. Six months or a year later, I probably would have taken it."

"And if Kyle takes it?"

"I'm going to die," she said, her lips quivering as she tried to hold back the tears.

"I'd hoped..." Noah began, then trailed off. He sighed. "I did warn you about him."

"I know." Amanda sniffed.

"Yeah." Noah nodded, his voice husky. "He has a way of getting past one's reservations. Something about the boy..."

The phone on Noah's desk buzzed. He grabbed the receiver. "Yeah?... I'll take it," he said, punching up another line. "Kyle," Noah mouthed to Amanda, swiveling in his chair.

Amanda rose from her chair, meaning to give Noah some privacy.

"You did, huh?" Noah's words stopped her in mid-stride. "I see. Well, congratulations. I'll see you when you get back, then."

Noah swiveled around to drop the earpiece in it's cradle. He looked over at Amanda.

"Well?"

"He said he wanted to talk to you himself."

"Noah . . ."

"He took it."

BY THAT NIGHT, the tissues in her pantry were long gone, but her tears weren't. She was reduced to using toilet tissue to dab her red, swollen eyes. She sat on the love seat, pretending to be invisible, wrapped in an old chenille robe that had never pretended to be stylish. In fact, it would look better on a bed, and the fuzzy slippers she wore on her feet would be better under a bed . . . way under.

Wiping her red nose again, she winced at it's tenderness. Her once bouncy curls moved droopily. Even her nails were a wreck; she'd been nervously picking the nail polish off them all day. She was a fine mess and proud of it. She was suffering in grand style. She looked down at her robe. Well, maybe *style* wasn't quite the right word.

She didn't even get up to answer the doorbell when it rang. Whoever it was would go away eventually, she hoped as she stared at the door.

As she watched, an envelope fell to the floor from the mail slot in the door.

Puzzled, the untucked her feet from beneath her and slowly got up to retrieve it. When she picked it up, her doorbell rang again. And again, before she could open the envelope.

Responding to the insistent appeal, she jerked open the door. "You!"

Kyle stood before her with an armful of white roses and a hopeful smile.

His eyes swept over her disheveled appearance, taking in her old robe and the crumpled tissues in her hand. "Oh, were you expecting someone else?" he asked, his blue eyes crinkling at the corners.

"I certainly wasn't expecting *you!*" she snapped, moving to slam the door in his face.

Kyle wedged his foot in the way, managing to thwart her effort to shut him out.

"I want you to leave," she demanded, sheer willpower alone keeping her tears at bay.

"No, you don't."

Amanda burst into tears. No, that was the awful part. She didn't want him to leave.

"What's all this?" he coaxed, pulling her into his arms and shoving the door closed with a backward kick.

"I turned down Westec's offer...so...so we could...and then you..." she sobbed.

"It's okay, baby," he said, rubbing his thumbs beneath her eyes to clear away her tears. "Look, I brought you roses," he said, handing them to her like some kind of peace offering.

Amanda brushed the roses away, scattering them to the floor. "I don't want your roses. I don't want anything from you. You took the offer from Westec after I turned it down to give us a chance together."

Kyle cocked his hip to one side and raised his fingertips to rest on his hips. "Of course I took the job. I'd be crazy not to. But I took it on the condition that Westec hire you as my cohost."

"You—you did?" she stammered. "You mean—"

"Don't you know by now that we're a team?" he asked, looking at her incredulously. "Don't you know I love you?"

Amanda hesitated, afraid to believe what he was telling her.

Kyle nodded to the envelope still in her hand. "If you're waiting for an *engraved invitation* . . ."

Amanda looked down at the envelope and then up at Kyle.

He nodded again.

She ripped open the envelope and pulled out the engraved card inside.

Amanda, love
Will you marry me? I promise to love, honor and ravish you.

Love always,
Kyle

Amanda's eyes started leaking again, only this time they were tears of happiness as she flew into Kyle's waiting embrace.

After a few moments, Kyle pulled back and looked down at her. "I take it that's a yes?"

Amanda nodded, still too choked up to speak.

Taking her hand, Kyle slipped a square-cut emerald engagement ring onto her wedding finger. "Under the light, it has the same fire as your eyes when we make love," he said, pulling her into his embrace once again to seal their betrothal with a passionate kiss.

When they came up for air, Amanda's eyes sparkled with happiness as she looked down at the engagement ring and then up at her new fiancé.

"I love you, Kyle Fox," she said, her voice full of wonder.

"And I love you," Kyle said, looking deep into her eyes.

Epilogue

AMANDA ENTERED the bedroom to start getting ready for her night on the town with Kyle to celebrate their wedding anniversary. She heard the shower running in the adjoining bath, and a smile of mischief lifted her lips. She was about to sneak in and join Kyle when her eye caught sight of the envelope on her pillow.

She reached for it with a knowing smile.

Stretching out across the bed, she pulled the pages of yellow legal paper from the envelope, Kyle's bold scrawl seducing her.

Amanda,

I thought you understood that as president of my own television syndicate, I'm a very important and powerful man, not to be trifled with. I'm a man used to having my wishes obeyed. And still you aren't ironing my shirts.

What's that? You refuse? Are you quite sure you want to do that?

You are? Then come to my office. I shall have to deal with you.

Come in, come in. Have a seat. I'll just be a moment while I tell my secretary to hold all my calls for the next hour.

Okay, now. Where were we? Oh yes, you were disobeying my wishes, weren't you? Do you really think that's wise?

You don't care, you're not ironing my shirts, no matter what? Hmm. . . . I see.

Do you see this necktie I'm undoing? Come here. No, turn around. That's it. Now put your hands together behind you.

There now, did I tie it too tight? You're not going to answer me, huh? Well, I'll be happy to untie them as soon as you decide you want to stop being so obstinate.

So, you're going to remain being stubborn, then?

Whew, is it hot in here? Do you feel warm? I do. I think I'll take off my jacket. There, that's much better. Maybe it's the sunlight coming in through the window that's making it so warm. I think I'll just close the blinds.

Gosh, that made it kind of dark, didn't it? I know, my desk lamp ought to be just about right. Okay, now come over here and sit on my knee. Careful. There, yes, that's it.

Now, do you see my shirt? It's a high-grade cotton with French cuffs and an English spread collar. I like a little starch in the collar, but I like the rest to be soft against my skin.

Here, let me take it off and rub it over your cheek so you can feel what I mean.

What are you staring at? Haven't you ever seen a man's bare chest before? Oh, I see. Not one like mine. Well, I do work out to keep in shape. I've been told women like a washboard belly. Is that why you're staring there?

If you were to promise you'd iron my shirts, I could untie your hands and you could touch me. I'd let you feel my hard muscles ripple beneath your fingertips.

How about it? Promise to iron my shirts?

No!

Okay. It's completely up to you, of course. I wouldn't want you to do anything you didn't want to do.

See this? Looks pretty hard, huh? Not a bad bicep for someone who wears a suit all week, is it?

Tell you what. Let me help you up here on my desk.

Comfortable? No, I can't untie your hands until you decide you want to iron my shirts. Maybe with a little encouragement, huh? What do you think?

Here, let me slide your high heels off and give you a foot massage. That's it. Set your foot right here on my lap. Feel that? It's not my bicep, is it?

Umm . . . maybe I could iron my own shirts . . . How about if I untie your hands? Do you think you could convince me that I'd rather send my shirts to the cleaner's and have you do something else for me with your time?

*You do? Oh, well, in that case . . . There. It's done. Let
me rub your wrists. I didn't have it tied too tight, did I?
Good.*

*Wait a minute. What are you doing? Aren't you wor-
ried you'll wrinkle your blouse, throwing it on the floor
like that?*

You don't care? Well, okay.

*Uh . . . your stockings, too? And your garter belt. . . .
Amanda, you're not wearing panties!*

*You know? Dear me. Uh . . . what's that? You want me
to come there? You mean you want to . . . on the desk!*

Well, I guess . . . Do you think? Really?

Amanda! That's my telephone receiver!

I'm coming, I'm coming. Put it down.

*Just let me get my pants off . . . and my shoes. Oh God,
Amanda, you drive me crazy. . . .*

Amanda smiled as she slipped the yellow legal pages
back into the envelope and slid it under her pillow.
Later she'd put it in the stack she kept tied with a ribbon in the locked drawer of her desk.

Looking up, she saw Kyle enter the room, a towel
slung low on his lean hips.

"You're incorrigible, you know," she said, kneeling
up on the bed and reaching for the towel anchored at
his waist.

"Not me." Kyle grinned. "You must be thinking of my evil twin, Lyle."

"Oh yes, Lyle," Amanda said, pulling him down onto the bed. "I was thinking about paying Lyle a little visit at his office tomorrow afternoon...say around threeish?"

"Umm, I guess that means I'm never going to get my shirts ironed?"

"Are you complaining?" She giggled as her mouth did wicked things.

"No ma'am...." Kyle answered, his words a strangled reply.

Have You Ever Wondered If You Could Write A Harlequin Novel?

Here's great news—Harlequin is offering a series of cassette tapes to help you do just that. Written by Harlequin editors, these tapes give practical advice on how to make your characters—and your story—come alive. There's a tape for each contemporary romance series Harlequin publishes.

Mail order only

All sales final

TO: *Harlequin Reader Service*
Audiocassette Tape Offer
P.O. Box 1396
Buffalo, NY   14269-1396

I enclose a check/money order payable to HARLEQUIN READER SERVICE® for $9.70 ($8.95 plus 75¢ postage and handling) for EACH tape ordered for the total sum of $_____ *
Please send:

- ☐ Romance and Presents
- ☐ American Romance
- ☐ Superromance
- ☐ Intrigue
- ☐ Temptation
- ☐ All five tapes ($38.80 total)

Signature_____
                                    (please print clearly)
Name:_____
Address:_____
State:_____ Zip:_____

*Iowa and New York residents add appropriate sales tax.

AUDIO-H